PERFECT MATCH

Pamela Toth

ZEBRA BOOKS
KENSINGTON PUBLISHING CORP.

ZEBRA BOOKS are published by

Kensington Publishing Corp.
850 Third Avenue
New York, NY 10022

First Zebra Printing: May, 1996
10 9 8 7 6 5 4 3 2 1

Printed in the United States of America

One

"Drop it." Erin McKenzie bent to take a sock from the black Lab standing before her in the paved exercise yard. "Good boy. Good Ranger." The dog wagged his long tail.

"He catches on fast," Anna, her partner at the training center said from where she sat watching Erin and Ranger work.

Erin knew Anna was right. At the speed Ranger was learning the advanced commands, he'd be ready for a human partner a month ahead of schedule.

"Lucy Blackwood called," Anna continued as Erin scratched behind Ranger's silky ears.

The yard where she'd led the dog through his paces was surrounded by single-storied buildings that were painted a cheery yellow and separated by wide paved walkways. The sky overhead was an incredible shade of blue, the weather unusually mild for October in the Northwest.

Erin pushed a hand through her heavy bangs, glad that her copper hair was short and bared the back of her neck to the faint breeze. The white sweatshirt and faded jeans she'd put on that morning were too warm.

"Lucy's still coming, isn't she?" Lucy Blackwood was scheduled in the next training group. She had been partially paralyzed in a car accident and wanted desperately to get a service dog.

"You bet. She called to say that her brother's driving her up from Eugene, and that she's looking forward to the class."

"That's good." Erin hadn't talked to Nick Blackwood yet, but she sensed from what Lucy had said and even more from what she hadn't that there was friction between her and her older brother.

"She's actually looking forward to boot camp." Anna shook her head, her expression incredulous.

"Sure," Erin agreed. "As much as anyone looks forward to a month of training and constant testing. Lucy's determined, though. I'll be surprised if she doesn't make it through." The training course that taught handicapped applicants how to work with service dogs was a real challenge. It had to be to make sure that each participant would get the most out of having a canine companion.

"Lucy sounded tense on the phone," Anna admitted. "I think she's more nervous about coming up here than she's willing to let on, perhaps even to herself."

"I'm looking forward to meeting her." Erin was always eager to meet the applicants. "I gather that her brother has money, but she still wants to be independent. I admire that. It would be so much easier for her to let him take care of her."

"If he's willing," Anna said.

Erin glanced at the dog that sat patiently beside her. "Ranger, kiss," she commanded, bending down. He licked her chin and she praised him again. "That's true," she agreed with Anna. "Maybe the man doesn't want a handicapped sister around anymore. A lot of people don't."

"Either way, I'm glad she's coming. I can't wait for the new group to get here. I love to see how much more self-confident they get as they start trusting their dogs."

Erin had begun to walk Ranger back to his kennel. At Anna's words she stopped and looked down at her friend. "I'm sure it'll work out, especially with the smaller group this time. It's too bad, though, that we're only taking three candidates and that one of the housing units will sit empty. I hate for that to happen with such a long waiting list for dogs."

"Me, too. But it's not your fault that Casey didn't work out." With a flick of her wrist, Anna spun her wheelchair so she could look Erin full in the face. "Be patient," she urged. "The program will grow. It just takes time."

"And lots of money," Erin added, sighing. Always money.

Anna's chuckle was slightly rueful. "Any place that runs on donations has to worry about money, and we sure run on donations, don't we?"

"You bet." Erin returned her smile. In the last year they'd raised a solid base of corporate funds, but they never had quite as much as they needed for the center's endless expenses, and she refused to raise the fee they charged the handicapped applicants. It was only a token payment but she didn't want anyone to go without a dog because they couldn't afford one.

"We always seem to find it when we need it," Anna reminded her. "But for now, I'd better make sure that Kim's got the units ready." She wheeled efficiently across the cement.

Erin stared after her for a moment, remembering how graceful and athletic Anna had been in college where the two of them had met and shared a dorm room their freshman year. Even now, Anna didn't need the chair all the time, but they both knew she would eventually.

"We're all done for today," Erin told the dog that still waited patiently at her side, dark eyes alert. "Ranger, heel."

She took the Lab back to the kennel area, pausing to praise and stroke him again before unsnapping his leash and releasing him into a spotlessly clean pen. Then she brought out the next dog to be worked, a border collie.

"Hi, Queenie." Erin bent to fondle the collie's floppy ears and fasten her leash.

Queenie's bushy tail wagged in enthusiastic response as she trotted beside Erin.

Nick Blackwood took his eyes off the road for a moment and glanced at his younger sister, who sat next to him in the luxurious interior of his Mercedes.

"You okay?" he asked, returning his attention to the expanse of highway that would eventually take them to the small town of Monroe in Northwestern Washington.

Lucy ended her silent contemplation of the surrounding countryside. "I'm a little nervous."

Nick was sure from the tension in her face that her admission was a gross understatement. Once she had hurled herself headlong into new experiences, but he knew it was much harder since she'd been confined to her chair.

"Everything will be okay," he tried to reassure her. "I'll bet everyone in the class is nervous at first." His heart ached for the energetic teenager whose life had been so drastically altered two years before. All the money and power behind the Blackwood name hadn't been enough to repair Lucy's injuries. Now she was placing her fragile hopes in this latest scheme, but Nick wondered how long she would stay with it. A butterfly was better at flitting from adventure to adventure than sticking to commitments. Even though the butterfly's wings had been abruptly clipped, Nick had seen nothing in the last two years to indicate that Lucy's basic nature had changed, not the programs she'd abandoned, the plans she'd quickly lost interest in or the parade of physical therapists she'd fired when they didn't show her immediate results.

"I know my life is going to change," she said now, voice vibrant with excitement. "As long as I can make it through the next four weeks and get a dog, I'll finally be able to live on my own."

Nick couldn't understand why Lucy wasn't content to continue living with him. His large house had more than enough room for her and as many trained attendants as she wanted. Instead of taking advantage of what his money could provide for her, Lucy was determined to go through this month-long training program at the center, learning to rely on an animal of questionable breeding and dubious capabilities.

Nick could see disappointment and possible disaster ahead. What could a dog hope to do for his sister that specially trained personnel couldn't?

He slapped the steering wheel, making Lucy jump. Her straight dark hair, a shade lighter than his own, swirled around her face as she tossed her head.

"Want to go home?" Nick asked quietly. "It's not too late to turn back."

Lucy's chin rose in that defiant gesture he knew all too well. "No."

He sighed. That would have been too easy. "What are you nervous about, peanut?" The nickname he'd used since he'd first seen her swaddled in a pink blanket came automatically to his lips.

"Everything." The hand that Lucy could still control made a helpless gesture. "What if the dog doesn't like me? What if I can't make him mind or I don't learn fast enough?"

Nick grinned. "Not like you? How could a dog not like someone who's going to spoil it rotten?"

Lucy's pretty face tightened into a mock grimace. "I'm not going to spoil him," she said. "He's going to be my companion, not just a pet like Sparky." Sparky was the basset hound that Nick had raised from a pup. There was no question that Sparky was spoiled.

Nick's growing exasperation was real. He knew Lucy was quoting from that McKenzie woman's pamphlet. She'd have a lot to answer for if his sister was disappointed.

"I can get you the best trained *human* companions," he insisted, renewing an old argument. "You don't need a dog for friendship."

"Companionship," Lucy corrected him. "And it's not just that. I want a service dog so I can be more independent."

"You don't need to knock yourself out trying to be more independent," Nick exclaimed, keeping his attention riveted on the road. He hated the idea that his beloved baby sister might try this new idea and fail. Better that she let *him* take care of her. He'd be more than happy to give her everything she could ever need. It was the least he could do. When Lucy didn't reply to his comment, he changed tactics.

"You know the house is plenty large enough for us to keep out of each other's way. I've even offered to build you an apartment on the grounds, if you want more privacy."

"Yeah," Lucy burst out, "an apartment for me and my human watch dog!"

Nick felt his temper rising. "Well, you can't live alone, can you? Who'd take care of you?" As always, Nick was frustrated and angry at Lucy's stubborn refusal to accept any more of his help than she had to. Didn't she understand that he only wanted what was best for her? Nothing he could ever do would cost too much or be too much trouble. She was his baby sister and she needed him. Whether or not she was prepared just now to admit it.

"I'm tired," Lucy said plaintively. "I'm going to rest." Her eyes closed abruptly. It was a ploy he knew she exercised frequently since it was often the only way she could escape him.

Nick glanced at his watch. "Yeah, take a little nap," he told her. "We should be getting there in about fifteen minutes." He glanced at her face, so serene in repose. "I love you," he added gruffly.

Her lips curved upward.

"So stop worrying. If that dog has any sense, he'll fall for you on first sight. And just to make sure, I'm going to be right there with you the whole time."

Lucy's eyes flew open. "What do you mean?" she demanded.

"I'm going to find a motel in Monroe so I can stay and help you with the course instead of going back home. I made arrangements at work." Nick knew he was doing the right thing.

Erin was in her apartment at the complex, feeding her cat, when she heard a car arriving. The day before the start of a new session was always exciting, meeting the students and assessing their ability to complete the training course and adjust to one of her dogs.

Giving Shiftless a last pat on his dark head, Erin left the cat lying in a patch of sunlight and went outside. A shiny black Mercedes had pulled up, and all she could see was the back of a dark-haired man as he bent to lift a folded wheelchair from the trunk. As Erin approached, absently admiring the span of the man's wide shoulders beneath his plaid shirt, he turned and set up the chair. Then he saw Erin and straightened. Despite his casual clothes, she guessed from the car he drove and the arrogant tilt to his head that he had to be Lucy's brother.

"Mr. Blackwood?" she asked, approaching him with her hand extended.

He nodded, watching her through narrowed eyes before he clasped her hand in his much larger one. His palm was hard with callouses.

"I'm Erin McKenzie. You and your sister are the first of the new class to arrive."

He remained silent. The lack of warmth in his smile as his gaze clashed with hers was a surprise. And a pity, since the rest of him was so attractive. The disapproval in the green-gold depths of his eyes did little to mar his appeal. Slightly flustered by her awareness of him as a man, Erin bristled as he abruptly released her hand.

"Miss McKenzie," he acknowledged finally in a voice as deep and sinfully compelling as dark chocolate. Then he reached to open the passenger door of the car. "My sister, Lucy."

Erin was relieved to transfer her attention to the girl waiting impatiently. Her eyes were direct, like her brother's, but her smile was edged with nervousness as she echoed his greeting.

"Please, call me Erin. Everyone does."

To her relief, Lucy's tentative smile widened. "Then you'd better call him Nick, or he'll forget you don't work for him and be handing you a hammer or a roll of blueprints."

Erin remembered that her father had told her Blackwood, Inc., was a power in commercial construction all down the Oregon coast. "Sounds like a hands-on contractor," she remarked.

"I am." He had moved the wheelchair and, to Erin's surprise, his firm mouth quirked slightly. "But there are probably a few people in the business who wish I weren't." Then, frowning as if he'd unwillingly dropped his guard, he turned toward his sister.

"I can get out by myself," she protested as Nick lifted her from the car.

"I don't mind helping," he said quietly.

Erin hoped there wasn't more to this situation than just an older brother's protectiveness. Surely Nick could understand that the more independent Lucy became, the better off she'd be.

When his sister was settled into her chair, Nick straightened, catching Erin's eye. She realized that she'd been staring. Every move he made radiated effortless strength.

"Let me show you to Lucy's quarters." She was feeling flustered that he'd caught her gawking.

"I wasn't expecting a facility like this," he told her. "You've got quite a set-up here."

Erin brought her attention sharply around to what he was saying. It wasn't like her to be so distracted, no matter how enticing the man.

"We're very proud of our center. A lot of dedicated people worked very hard to make *Northwest Service Dogs* into what you see now. And we're growing all the time." Hearing the pomposity of her words, Erin ducked her head. "Sorry." She couldn't help smiling. "I get carried away sometimes."

Lucy had been turning slowly in her wheelchair, looking at the cluster of neatly painted buildings, sunny yellow with white trim. Around each were borders of vibrant, late-blooming chrysanthemums. "I can hardly believe I'm here."

Erin squatted beside her chair, glad to shift her attention away from Nick. "I'm glad you came. Let's get you settled and then I'll give you the fifty-cent tour."

"Fifty cents?" Nick echoed. "Isn't that kind of high?"

Erin straightened and sent him what was meant to be a cheeky grin before she picked up one of the bags he'd unloaded from the trunk. "This place doesn't run on good intentions," she admitted, "so we never miss a chance to solicit donations." She glanced at Lucy. "Follow me. I'll show you where you'll be staying."

For a moment, Nick stood motionless as he watched Erin walk away. This set-up wasn't anything like he'd pictured, and neither was its director. Instead of a solid, middle-aged matron with iron gray hair, stout shoes and a cause, Ms. McKenzie was a young, red-haired moppet with freckles and one hell of an attractive butt in snug, faded jeans. Nick couldn't help but wonder why such a pretty, vital female was content to bury herself in a small town like Monroe, doing the work she did.

Erin glanced behind her before she rounded the corner to be sure they were both coming. The whole complex was adapted for wheelchair access but she knew how daunting the first day could be for people who were the most comfortable with familiarity and routine. She saw Nick pick up the remaining bag and begin to follow his sister, his expression thoughtful.

Erin stopped before the door of Lucy's unit and pushed on the handle to open it. That type of entry was easier to manipulate than a knob.

"Here we are." She stepped aside to let Lucy precede her.

"Can you recommend a good motel in town?" Nick asked. "I've decided to stick around while Lucy takes your course."

Surprised, Erin turned to study his face. It was too weathered to be strictly handsome, but the sum of his individual features managed to be both strong and appealing. She thought she saw a hint of vulnerability in his green eyes, but it was gone before she could be sure.

"You know it's not really necessary that you stay," she told him. "I understand you have a business to run back home."

"I've made arrangements," he said in a tone as plain as a "keep out" sign. "I'm going to be here for Lucy. In case she needs anything." His gaze flickered to his sister and then back to Erin. "I don't intend to get in your way."

A man like you wouldn't be able to help it, she thought with irreverence. It was clear that Nick was used to being in charge and, if she wasn't mistaken, he cared very much for his sister. Whether or not that would be *good* for Lucy remained to be seen.

"You can stay right here if you'd like," Erin found herself offering. "We're short a dog this session. That makes us short one applicant, too, so we have an empty unit. You can stay next door to Lucy. We even provide meals."

Nick reached toward his back pocket. "I'll pay extra, of course."

Erin raised a detaining hand, wondering if she was making a huge mistake in letting him stay. "That's not necessary." He looked ready to argue, so she thought quickly. "If you're willing, I'm sure that Darren, who does the maintenance, can always use an extra pair of hands." Perhaps he could keep Nick so busy he wouldn't have time to interfere with his sister's training.

Nick didn't ask who Darren was. Instead, he appeared to consider her offer. "You sure?" he asked, as he let his hand drop to his side. "I didn't expect you to put me up."

Erin shrugged. "The unit's not fancy. It'll sit empty if you don't take it. And what's another potato in the soup?"

He looked at Lucy, who was in the doorway of her unit. "What do you think?"

She didn't meet his gaze and her tone was sullen when she said, "You're going to do what you want anyway."

Erin experienced a flash of regret for extending the invitation. It sounded to her as if Lucy was used to losing arguments to her older brother. Erin was tempted to say something but long experience made her hold her tongue. They'd have to work this out themselves.

"Here's the other unit," she said instead, opening the door next to Lucy's. "They all look about the same." Only the doorways and bathrooms had been adapted for wheelchair access. Applicants and their dogs were expected to cope with otherwise normal surroundings.

"Sure I can't find a motel?" Nick asked after he'd glanced inside at the neat but Spartan bed-sitting room.

Erin's smile was deliberately bland. "If it's okay with Lucy, it's okay with me." She noticed that he didn't ask his sister again. Instead, he set down the bag he'd been holding and went into the second unit.

Erin turned back to Lucy, who was still waiting. "Let me show you where everything is," she offered, hefting the bag.

"I didn't know until we were halfway here that he planned to stay," Lucy said in a subdued voice while Erin was showing her the intercom by the bed. "He's afraid I'd screw up on my own."

Erin raised her brows. "Maybe he just wants to lend you moral support."

Lucy didn't argue. Instead she wheeled her chair around. "This place will be okay," she said in a flat voice.

Before Erin could think of anything else to add, Nick knocked on the open door and came in.

"Everything okay?" Erin asked him.

For a moment, his gaze held hers. "Just fine. Thanks again."

"No problem." She hoped fervently that her words didn't prove to be untrue. "Dinner's at six every evening in the dining hall. The other two participants should be here by then. Breakfast's at seven-thirty and class starts at eight sharp." She smiled at Lucy. "Don't be late. There are maps of the complex in both your rooms and if you need anything, use the intercom. An attendant is always available. Feel free to look around if you aren't too tired. There isn't anyplace here that's off limits and one of us is usually close by if you have questions."

"Thanks." Lucy looked as if she were beginning to relax a little.

Erin didn't want her overextending herself. "You had a long drive. There's time to rest before dinner, if you'd like."

Lucy smiled and more animation filled her face. "The drive wasn't too bad. My brother's good company when he wants to be." She sent a teasing glance toward Nick. He grinned back and Erin noticed again how attractive he could be.

She wondered once more if his presence was going to be a help to Lucy or a hindrance. So much would depend on his attitude.

"If you need anything, just buzz." She started to leave.

"When can I meet my dog?" Lucy's tone was a mixture of excitement and caution.

Erin had to grin. The first thing everyone who came here wanted was to meet their dog. "We won't actually make the permanent assignments until about the third day, but the dogs are all in their pens now, if you want to get a look at them."

"I'd love to." Lucy nodded eagerly.

"Perhaps your brother would like to go with us?" Erin invited. Lucy spoke for him. "Sure, he would. Come on, Nick."

"Okay," he agreed, surprising Erin with a grin of shared amusement. "Let's go."

She led them past the dining hall and the main meeting room to the kennels. Hearing their approach, all the dogs were at the doors of their runs, tails wagging. She introduced them as Lucy wheeled forward and stuck her fingers out to be licked and sniffed.

"Oh, this one's pretty," she exclaimed over Ranger, the black labrador retriever.

Nick was watching her as she scratched the dog's head through the wire mesh. He didn't say anything, nor did he lean forward to touch any of the animals himself. Erin wondered what he was thinking.

"Ranger's one of the dogs we'll be working with tomorrow," she told Lucy. "Along with Queenie and Max."

"What about the rest of them?" Nick asked. The sudden intrusion of his deep voice made Erin tense up. Some instinct kept urging her to be on her guard with him.

"They aren't fully ready to be companion dogs yet. We're still working with them."

"Do you breed them here?" Lucy asked.

"No, we have breeders who donate them and puppy trainers who take them when they're weaned. The trainers keep them for a year, teaching them basic commands and getting them socialized. Then we train them for five to six more months here before they're ready for service."

"Wow," Lucy said, as a chocolate Lab named Bo licked her hand. "I didn't realize how complicated it is."

"Training takes a long time. That's one reason why we have such a waiting list." Erin glanced at Nick, but he didn't say anything, just watched his sister. Then Erin heard whistling as a man in coveralls rounded the corner, carrying a paint can and a brush.

"Darren," she exclaimed, almost relieved at the intrusion. "I'd like you to meet two of our new guests, Lucy Blackwood and her brother, Nick. This is Darren Girrard. His wife is my business partner. Darren is the one who gets the credit for keeping this place in such good shape."

There were general greetings and hand shakes, and then Darren returned his attention to Erin. She thought there were new lines around his eyes, but she didn't comment. Perhaps Anna was feeling worse.

"Where's your wife?" Erin asked.

Darren tilted his head in the direction of the office. "Where do you think?" Then he headed toward the small storage and shop building set behind the others. "See you all at dinner," he called, waving the paint brush.

"That's the man you said would be glad of my help," Nick commented. "I'm beginning to understand why."

"Smart fella," Erin told him. "Now, if you two can find your way back to your rooms, I'd better make sure Anna isn't overdoing it again. She keeps the books and handles all the correspondence, but sometimes she forgets the time when she's in front of the computer screen."

The other two applicants, an older woman who was replacing a service dog that had died, and a young boy with muscular dystrophy, both arrived while Erin was in the office with Anna. After they settled into their assigned units, everyone got acquainted over dinner. They were all still sitting at a long table when Erin excused herself to check on the dogs one last time.

"I'll see you all tomorrow," she said to the group as she grabbed her jacket. "If you need anything after your attendant leaves tonight, be sure to use the intercom by your bed. Don't forget, breakfast is promptly at seven-thirty. And tomorrow will be a very full day, so get some rest."

"Miss McKenzie."

Erin heard the familiar voice as she left the dining hall. A flutter of anticipation surprised her as she turned and saw Nick coming after her, thrusting his arms into a light gray windbreaker that made his hair look blacker than midnight. He'd been quiet at dinner, not saying much except to answer a direct question or murmur something to his sister. Still, Erin had been aware of his presence the whole time she fielded questions and listened to the other people at the long table. Now she waited, curious as to what he might want.

"Could I talk with you for a minute?" he asked, the chiseled bones of his lean face prominent beneath the outdoor light as he towered over her own medium height. His voice was rich with the subtle shadings of self-confidence and Erin knew that he expected her to accede to his request. Perversely, she was tempted to plead some excuse and hurry off. The very childishness of the impulse surprised her.

"I'm going to check on the dogs," she told him as he began to walk with her in the direction of the kennels. "You're welcome to come along."

"Thanks." He didn't venture anything more during the short walk, and he remained quiet while Erin greeted each dog and made sure it had enough water for the night. She wondered if Nick thought her overly solicitous of the animals. Aside from the fact that she was fond of them all, each dog had a great deal of training time invested in it.

As soon as Erin realized what she was doing, her silent justifications made her wonder why Nick's presence was causing her to question nearly everything she did or said.

"How's Lucy getting along so far?" she asked to break the silence between them as she turned away from the last pen. The pool of light that illuminated the two of them was surrounded by darkness, giving her the odd feeling of being somehow isolated from the rest of the compound.

"She's doing okay, I guess." He shoved his hands into his back pockets and turned to stare into the night.

"What was it you wanted to talk about?" she asked, puzzled by his silence.

There was something solid, almost reassuring, about the strength of his profile. The image of a man to be counted on when the going got rough. Except that Erin couldn't allow herself that luxury.

"Is there anything about the training course or the dogs that you don't understand?" she prodded again when he didn't answer. "I'm sure that Lucy will do fine, if you're worried about her. She's a good candidate, young, bright and eager. The use of her good hand and arm will make things easier for her, too."

Nick turned to look at Erin, and she took an involuntary deep breath.

"I'm sure you'll be pleased with what Lucy and her dog can accomplish together," she added. The sudden realization that she was chattering so fast that he couldn't have gotten a question in if he'd wanted to made her stop abruptly. She was waiting for some response from him when he finally sighed and looked away. If anything, his expression had only grown more distant.

"There's one thing you need to understand about Lucy," he said, voice low and determined. He hesitated again. "I love my sister, don't get me wrong. She's over twelve years younger than me, and sometimes she seems more like my daughter." He stopped again, as if groping for words. Finally he rubbed a hand over his face.

"Lucy can be flighty," he said finally. "She doesn't always stick to things. Even as a young child, she was always looking for the next toy, the next treat."

Erin tried to nod understandingly, but she didn't think Nick really noticed.

"In the two years since her accident, she's started and stopped several therapy programs, gone through a slew of attendants—"

"You think she'll quit the course," Erin guessed, interrupting him. "You think she won't succeed in getting a canine companion, and that will be one more disappointment for her."

Nick's eyes were dark with shadows. He looked younger, more vulnerable. "Yeah," he agreed. "One more failure, for a girl who's had more than her share of failures in the last couple of years. And, even if she does stay with your program, I don't see how getting a dog can fulfill all her expectations." He made a gesture with his hand. "She thinks a companion dog will change her life."

Erin's smile was relaxed. "Trust me," she said with a glow of confidence. "If Lucy completes the course and passes the tests, getting a companion dog *will* change her life. And change it for the better. Everyone here has a stake in her success, and we'll be doing all we can to help her. It's true that only Lucy, herself, can actually complete the training, but I have no reason to think she won't be successful. Then she'll be able to attain some of that independence she wants so badly."

To Erin's dismay, instead of relaxing a little of its anxiety, Nick's face twisted into an expression of vicious self-loathing. His reply shocked her further.

"Yeah, independence from *me*," he said bitterly, jabbing his chest with one finger. "Freedom from the bastard who put her into that damned wheelchair in the first place."

Two

Erin stared at Nick as shock ran through her. "You were driving the car?" she asked, aware of the waves of pain that radiated from him like an invisible force field.

His nod was abrupt, the expression on his attractive face shutting down as if he already regretted telling her. "Yes."

"I'm sorry." She didn't know what else to say. She couldn't very well ask if the accident was his fault. It must have been, for him to feel so strongly.

While she was fighting the totally unacceptable urge to put her arms around him in comfort, Nick looked away, as if he were searching the night for answers. "I'm going to make it up to her," he vowed in a low voice. "As much as I can, anyway. Lucy doesn't need a dog. She needs someone, a person she loves and trusts, to stand by her. *I'm* going to be that person, for as long as she needs me."

"You're wrong about the dog," Erin felt compelled to tell him. "I hope you'll give us a chance to show you what a companion dog can do for Lucy." A chilling thought struck her. "You aren't planning to interfere with her training, are you?" She waited for his answer, determined to keep arguing as long as necessary. Sometimes the handicapped people's relatives wanted to take care of them as a way to appease their own guilt, but Erin knew that nothing else took the place of the independence each individual could attain. Nick had to understand that up front.

"I won't interfere," he finally agreed. "But I'm not building up false hopes in Lucy either. I know what's best for my own sister, and I'll be here, waiting, when this idea falls through."

Erin bit her tongue. His determined tone made her decide reluctantly that further arguing right now was probably pointless. "I'd better let you go in," she said instead. "I've still got a few things to take care of, and tomorrow will be a full day for all of us."

If Nick was surprised at her failure to defend her program, he gave no sign. Instead, he bade her a quiet good night and turned away.

Erin watched him go. Despite his air of solitude, his broad shoulders were squared beneath his jacket and his head was high. She had an idea that the burden of guilt he carried was terribly heavy, just the same. And she wondered if he would overcome that guilt, deserved or otherwise, or if it would ultimately destroy him.

Erin headed for her own apartment with a sigh. How Nick Blackwood dealt with his guilt wasn't her problem. Her only concern should be whether Lucy completed the course and proved herself ready for a service dog. The other issue was one the girl and her brother would have to work out between them.

The next day brought with it a gray sky so pale it was almost colorless, an inconsistent breeze too weak to be considered a real wind and a cool but hardly unpleasant temperature. At least it wasn't raining, either a heavy, saturated mist that soaked everything or the steady downpour that could last for days at a time.

Erin had already spent a half hour with one of the less advanced dogs and was sitting in the dining hall enjoying a mug of coffee with Anna and Darren when the three eager students wheeled in, talking excitedly. They were followed by their attendants and Nick Blackwood.

"I can't wait to get started," Lucy carolled amidst the general greetings. Erin noticed that Nick moved closer to his sister's side and put a hand on her shoulder.

"Better have some breakfast first," Anna advised, catching Erin's nod of approval. They both knew that this first morning's enthusiasm would soon convert to complaints and groans of frustration over the next few days. Mixed, they hoped, with a growing spirit of teamwork and trust between each human-canine pairing—if all went well and *if* the three candidates were willing to work and study hard.

Erin found herself watching Nick's sister, looking for visible flaws that would betray a lack of commitment. Catching herself, she turned her attention to Nick, as if she expected to see his handsome features tainted with guilt. Instead, his expression was bland, almost indifferent as he met Erin's gaze, nodded and then let his attention wander on.

For a moment, she wondered how he managed to live with his guilt.

"You okay?" Anna asked her in an undertone.

Blinking, Erin nodded and turned her gaze to Jane, the older woman who had lost her previous service dog. Jane, who had been injured in a skiing accident years before, pulled her chair up next to Erin and began unloading her breakfast from a tray.

"I hope I can get another labrador," Jane said. "Dottie was such a good dog with the sweetest disposition. I had her for eight years."

"We've got one Lab, a golden retriever and a border collie ready for this class," Erin told her. "But don't judge your new dog by Dottie. Each companion is an individual, you know, just like people."

Jane smiled but her eyes, behind thick glasses, were full of tears. "I know," she said quietly, ducking her head. "I'll try."

"That's the spirit." Erin smiled her approval, then swallowed the rest of her coffee as she turned her thoughts to what lay ahead.

The first day would consist of an overview of the course and its goals, an introduction to the dogs and the start of actual training. They had a lot of material to cover and there wasn't any time to waste.

At the end of each day's lesson, there would be questions and review. The dogs already knew sixty-five commands; the humans had to learn them, too. Then the basics would be combined and customized to meet individual needs.

Erin glanced up and her gaze met that of Lucy's brother. For a moment his stare held hers immobile; then it shifted as he moved along in the breakfast line behind Lucy and her attendant.

Shaken by the chill in his eyes, Erin toyed with her eggs.

"Eat your breakfast before it gets cold," Anna nagged. She was always looking out for Erin. If only Anna would follow her own advice and take better care of herself.

Erin thought about saying as much, but then one of the attendants asked her a question and the moment was lost. As soon as the rest of the group was finished eating, she disposed of her own half-full plate and led the students to the practice room where Darren was waiting with three eager dogs on leashes. They wore bright orange working harnesses equipped with special saddlebags.

Darren gave Queenie, the border collie, to the young boy whose name was Fred. He immediately began to touch and talk to Queenie, while her tail signalled her pleasure. Max, a golden retriever, went to Jane.

"I'd rather have the Lab," she told Darren. "That's what I'm used to."

"You know these assignments aren't permanent," he reminded her. "You'll have a chance to work with each dog before we decide."

After a moment, Jane took Max's leash, extending her free hand for him to sniff and lick.

Ranger, the black Lab Jane had been eyeing, went to Lucy. She promptly bent forward to hug his neck with her good arm.

"That's right," Erin said, watching them. "Make friends with your dog. You'll each work with all three before we make the permanent assignments, probably a couple days from now. These dogs have been specially chosen as companions because they're smart, patient, strong and eager to please. So let them know when they're doing a good job, discipline them firmly but never harshly when necessary and they'll love you all the more."

She paused, looking at the three unusual couples before her, then glancing at Nick, who stood by Lucy's chair. While everyone was busy getting to know their dog, she motioned him aside.

"You're welcome to watch the training sessions," she told him in an undertone. "You can go on the field trips with us, too, as long as you don't interfere with the class."

His thick brows rose. "Interfere?" His tone made Erin's cheeks grow warm.

"I'm sorry," she said, silently conceding the round. "Perhaps that's too strong a word. What I mean is that Lucy has to complete the training course on her own. You can't help her."

His expression hardened. "Why not?"

"Lucy has to be able to command her dog's respect and control his obedience by herself. I know you have her best interests at heart, but if you try to make things easier for Lucy, in the long run you'll only make them harder. Unless we're sure that she can take care of her service dog and derive real benefit from it, she won't pass the course and she'll leave here empty-handed."

Nick shifted until he was leaning one broad shoulder against the wall. "This okay?" he asked.

Erin gave him a dry smile, determined not to let his attitude rile her. "Fine." She returned her attention to the students. All three were talking to their dogs, whose tails wagged in unison.

"Well, class," Erin said, raising her voice as she determined to ignore Nick's presence, "we have a lot to cover today. Throughout the course, we'll be learning commands, taking the dogs on outings to the mall in Everett, to the movies and to several restaurants. One of the other handlers or I will also work with you individually. There will be questions and review at the end of each day and then a quiz the next morning."

She paused to glance at the eager expressions on her students' faces. "Of course, you can ask questions at any time. When the four weeks are up, there will be a written test and a practical working exam in one of the public settings we've visited." She smiled at the looks of sudden apprehension. "Don't worry. After all that is graduation. We'll talk more about it later. For now let's get started."

From his spot by the wall, Nick watched Erin as she worked with the students. Her patience amazed him. The dogs, though obviously well-trained, were excited and confused by their new masters. Fred, the boy with muscular dystrophy, had a short attention span, but Erin repeated her instructions to him tirelessly, and waited while he tried to follow them.

"Am I next?" Lucy asked, glancing at Nick, who was still standing by the wall.

"Sure," Erin told her. "Just keep working on what I showed you until I'm finished with Fred. Let Ranger help you. Remember, he already knows a lot of what you have to learn."

"Okay." Lucy looked at Nick again, and he was tempted to go over and help her. It wasn't easy for him to stay where he was, merely sending her what he hoped was a reassuring smile instead.

Then his gaze wandered back to Erin, who had bent over to adjust Queenie's harness. Her shapely behind and long, slim legs were faithfully outlined in her snug, bleached jeans. While he continued admiring her posterior, Erin straightened. Jane said something to her and she glanced over her shoulder. Her gaze locked with Nick's and he watched the color climb her cheeks. Unable to pretend he'd been doing anything other than what he had, he wiggled his brows in an expression of approval. To his amusement, Erin's frown deepened, as did her blush.

Perhaps she wasn't as indifferent as she would have liked him to think.

Then Erin whirled and raised her voice. "Class, I think it's time we went outside."

Nick followed the ragged group to the training area at a safe distance. For the remainder of the morning, as the students practiced having the dogs pull them in their chairs, turning left or right and stopping, Lucy was the only one who even glanced in Nick's direction.

"I could use your help for a while this afternoon if you have some time."

Nick's attention shifted from his tuna sandwich to Darren, who stood beside the table.

"Erin said to ask you," the other man continued, shoving his hands into stained khaki work pants.

Nick glanced at Erin down at the other end of the table, but she was leaning forward, listening intently to something Fred was trying to tell her.

"Go ahead," Lucy said from her place at Nick's elbow. "I can get along without you for a couple of hours."

Nick hesitated. Was this her way of needling him for watching her class all morning? As many times as she'd looked his way, he'd thought she liked having him there.

"You'll be okay?" he asked.

Lucy rolled her eyes and made a face. "Yes. I'll be fine." She turned her attention to Darren. "He'd brush my teeth if I let him," she confided with a flirtatious smile.

"He only wants to help," Darren replied mildly. "I was the same way with my wife for a while."

Lucy glanced down the table. "Anna, right? Erin's partner."

Darren nodded. Nick noticed the way his expression softened as he followed the direction of Lucy's gaze.

Before she could ask any prying questions, Nick spoke up. "It looks like I've got the afternoon free," he told the other man. "What are we going to be doing?"

"Putting up storm windows. Four hands will make it a lot easier."

"When do we start?" Nick asked, beginning to rise.

Darren put a detaining hand on his shoulder. "Finish your lunch. Anna needs a little help in the office first, so I'll meet you in front of the shop in, say, a half hour. Okay?"

When Nick agreed, Darren wished Lucy luck with her class. Nick watched him move to where Anna was sitting. A smile of welcome broke across her face and Nick found himself envying the two of them. He'd had relationships, but not one whose breakup he really regretted. Maybe if a woman had smiled at him in just that way—

Allowing the thought to drift away, he noticed that Erin was watching him with a thoughtful expression. She didn't seem pleased when Nick saluted her with half his tuna sandwich. He needed to remember that his sister was the most important woman in his life now. There wasn't room for anyone else and he certainly didn't need the distraction that a romantic involvement would surely create, he reminded himself ruthlessly as he bit into the tuna, which he despised.

Again, Nick's attention slid without his consent to Erin's enticing figure as she stood and paused to say something to Jane before carrying her dishes to the tub by the kitchen doorway. He hoped that Darren was a slave driver. Perhaps an afternoon of physical labor would cure Nick of the restlessness that had gripped him since his arrival at the center.

"Anna's been in remission for over a year now," Darren said as the two men lifted another storm window. Nick held it steady while Darren secured it in place. "We're hoping it lasts forever."

"I hope it does, too," Nick said as they lifted another window. "Anna seems like a real nice woman."

"Oh, she is." For a moment, Darren's ready grin wavered. "She and Erin were college roommates when Anna got sick." He positioned the frame over the existing window. "I think that was a deciding factor in Erin starting this center. She'd been planning to become a veterinarian."

Nick hid his surprise. He hadn't thought about her doing something else, having ordinary plans for the future. In his mind he'd linked her to the center, like a nun with the Church. He shifted restlessly. Thinking about Erin as he might about any other woman with feelings and dreams, wants and needs, made him desperately uncomfortable. Made him imagine her in ways he hadn't any right to.

Ways his imagination insisted on picturing in lurid detail.

"How'd you and Anna meet?" he asked Darren, to change the subject.

There was no way around it. Erin missed knowing that Nick was somewhere close by, watching what she was doing. Perhaps he'd only been there to keep tabs on his sister, but Erin was forced to admit, at least to herself, that she didn't mind having him around nearly as much as she'd thought she would. If she wasn't careful, she'd be eagerly looking forward to seeing his shadowed face and tall, commanding frame. She'd be distracted, like she was now.

"Is this right?" Jane's question about the exercise she was practicing with Max, having him position himself so she could grasp his harness and have him pull her chair, brought Erin immediately back to the present.

"Let me see you do it again," she told the older student, watching carefully while Jane put the golden retriever through his paces.

Jane's eyes were anxious as she looked up for approval. Erin had an idea how much getting a new dog meant to her, after becoming accustomed to the relative freedom she'd had with Dottie.

"Yes, you've got the idea. Just run through it a couple more times to get Max used to minding you. You know the more the two of you work together, the smoother a team you'll be."

"Okay," Jane agreed cheerfully. Either she'd discovered that Labs weren't the only satisfactory service dogs or she was just biding her time until her turn to work with Ranger; Erin wasn't sure which.

Determined to keep her mind on her work, Erin turned to Fred to see how he and Queenie were doing. Everything was harder for the boy to master, both because of his youth and short attention span and because he was severely handicapped. But he was a bright, willing pupil and Erin didn't think he'd fail. It was students like Fred who made her job especially rewarding.

His parents had driven him over from Spokane. His mother wanted to stay with him, but there were three more children at home. Erin had an idea how hard it had been for her and Fred's father to leave him there, and she knew they called frequently.

For a moment, she was lost in thought, but then Fred said something and it took all of Erin's concentration to understand his slowly enunciated words.

The next afternoon, Nick was dealing with his memories the way he always did, by shoving them aside and, if that didn't cut it, with hard physical labor.

"Hey, don't work so fast or you'll make me look bad." Darren came around the side of the building, pushing a wheelbarrow.

Nick was pruning a row of dead-looking fuschia bushes that would send up new shoots in the spring. Startled, he glanced around to see that he was almost done. Piles of withered branches surrounded him. He made a vague gesture with the pruning shears.

"No point in wasting time."

For a moment, he was the uncomfortable subject of Darren's considering stare.

"Living with someone who has limitations like Anna and Lucy is never easy," Darren said as he began to load the dead branches into the wheelbarrow. "If you ever want to talk, I'm a pretty good listener."

His offer surprised Nick, who'd learned at an early age to keep his feelings to himself. More than once, his father had told him a real man didn't whine about what life dealt him. He just played the hand and carried on.

"Thanks," he said hesitantly. "I don't have any problems with Lucy's handicap, but thanks for offering."

Darren shrugged, his grin easy. "Sure. Now, since you're done here, why don't you put all these branches on the pile out back while I go unstop the sink in the main kitchen? After we mow and trim the grass in the front, we'll be done for today."

Nick uttered a groan. "Slave driver," he accused mockingly. "I don't work this hard at my own business."

With a chuckled "better get used to it," Darren left him.

It was later, while Nick was edging the grass along one of the paved pathways, that he saw Erin talking to Darren, who was running the mower. Darren shut off the machine, glanced at Nick, and then gestured to the wide expanse of lawn still to be cut.

Apparently, Erin didn't like whatever Darren was telling her. Nick could see her frown from where he stood watching discreetly. She finally shrugged and whirled toward Nick.

He lowered his head and resumed his task, not stopping until she called his name over the noise of the gas-driven trimmer.

"Could I talk to you for a minute?" she shouted when he straightened.

Nick tried to prepare himself for the jolt her bright blue eyes and soft mouth always sent through him. Today she looked more attractive than usual in snug tan jeans and an emerald green tee-shirt that paid unabashed homage to her red hair. Awareness hit Nick like a blow to the solar plexis.

He switched off the trimmer. "What is it?" His voice sounded harsher than he'd intended.

Erin colored slightly. "Darren usually goes into town with me to pick up the dog food, but for some reason he wants to finish the lawn right now. "We buy it in hundred pound bags, and I wondered if you'd mind—"

Sorry he'd sounded so grumpy, Nick quickly said, "Sure, I'll go with you. When do you want to leave?"

"Right away." Her eyes were unreadable.

For a moment, he allowed himself the luxury of returning her stare, wondering what had put the shadows in her eyes. Or who. He pulled his damp tee-shirt away from his chest.

"Let me change and I'll be right with you."

"Meet me by the vans," she said, turning away. Then she glanced back over her shoulder and smiled. "Thanks."

"How far to the feed store?" Nick asked idly as the van rolled down the highway toward Snohomish.

"Five more minutes." Erin was too aware of him sitting beside her in the confines of the van. Now that she had him alone, she might as well bring up something she felt needed to be said. Their gazes met, lingered, and then she broke away. He'd changed to a plaid flannel shirt in shades of gray that made his green eyes shimmer. Its long sleeves were rolled back from his muscular forearms and Erin couldn't help but notice the dusting of black hair on his tanned skin. What was it about this man that brought her to almost painful awareness? She'd been attracted to other men, but not like this. When Nick was around she felt like an adolescent with a crush.

And overactive hormones.

"I need to talk to you about your sister," she blurted to halt the direction of her thoughts.

Nick sat up straighter and impaled her with his stare, which had changed to green ice. "Is something wrong?"

Erin hesitated. Too late to back off now.

"I can't really put my finger in it," she admitted finally as she signalled and turned off the busy highway. "It's her attitude in class. I know she really wants to succeed, but she's, well, distracted." Erin swallowed as she turned another corner. "I think it's your presence that's bothering her."

"My presence?" he echoed. "I wasn't even there this afternoon."

"I know." Erin hesitated, then went on doggedly. "And I think she missed you, which isn't good. She can't be too dependent on you or she won't succeed with her dog. I know you mean well, but she needs self-assurance now, not on-site support."

For a moment, Nick looked as if he were struggling with his temper. Then he took a deep breath.

"What does Lucy have to say about this?"

Erin studied the road. "I haven't spoken to her yet. I wanted to talk to you first." She pulled up in front of the feed store, backed expertly into a parking spot and cut the motor, but made no move to open the door. Now that she'd started this discussion, she wanted to get it finished. She needed to see it through, for Lucy's sake.

Pamela Toth

"I think it might be best if you considered leaving for the rest of the course."

Dead silence met her suggestion. The only sign Nick gave that he'd even heard her was the bunching of his dark brows.

"Best for who?" he asked when she thought the silence was going to last forever. "Lucy or you?"

"I beg your pardon?"

Nick leaned closer. Erin could see shards of gold in his green eyes. They were framed by short, thick lashes. "I think you know what I mean." His voice had dropped to a husky whisper and his gaze settled on her mouth.

Erin's whole body jolted with surprise as her stunned brain absorbed the meaning of his question. Heat rose in her cheeks and she straightened away from him. Had he seen the attraction she felt toward him?

"You've gotten the wrong idea," she sputtered, trying to ignore her own leaping reaction to his intense scrutiny. "I would never let personal feelings get involved." She should have discarded Darren's suggestion that she bring Nick with her.

Nick's gleaming eyes narrowed. "So you admit to personal feelings?" he asked.

"Of course not. That's not what I meant at all." Erin knew she had two choices, either get out of the van *now* or possibly make things even worse. "I'm going to get the dog food," she said in her chilliest voice. "You can help me or not. Frankly, right now I don't really care which."

Before she could escape the close confines of the van, Nick wrapped his fingers around her upper arm, effectively holding her in place.

"Let me go," she ordered him, acutely aware of the warmth from his touch burning through her sleeve.

"In a minute. First I think we need to clear up a little something between us."

"I can clear it up just fine without you manhandling me," Erin said through gritted teeth as she tried with little success to hold onto her rapidly shredding control. "You're *way* out of line."

Nick's gaze held hers as effectively as the tractor beam in a Star Trek rerun. "Prove it," he challenged.

"Prove it?" Erin echoed, as Nick's closeness fueled her unwilling fascination. "How?"

Something flashed in his eyes and then was gone before she could read it. "Kiss me."

Three

Although Nick's face didn't show it, he was almost as startled by his suggestion that Erin kiss him as she so obviously was. It was true that he'd been drawn to her since they'd first met, but he'd had no intention of acting on that attraction. Nor did he intend to go home to Eugene as she wanted him to. Not without Lucy. Instead of thinking about why it was so important that he stay, Nick gazed intently at Erin to see what she would do. He didn't have long to wait.

"Kiss you?" she sputtered. "I'd rather kiss a pig!" She lifted her chin and looked down her nose at Nick. The fair skin of her cheeks was now a vibrant pink and her bright hair almost crackled with indignation.

"Ouch," he exclaimed with a wince. She was really something when she was angry. Explosive. Seductive. "No need to be so cruel."

"How dare you accuse me of putting my own interests ahead of those of my students," she continued as if she hadn't heard him. "Just because *you* refuse to see the need for my service dogs, doesn't mean that *I* take my commitments lightly."

Nick studied her with care, fascinated by her burst of temper. Then he sobered abruptly. What was he doing, indulging himself like this? He was here for Lucy, not to flirt with Ms. McKenzie.

"If you're waiting for me to kiss you, I'm afraid you're in for a very long wait," Erin told him, reaching behind her to open the door of the van. "And the nights can get pretty chilly around here this time of year."

Before Nick could utter a word in his own defense, Erin hurried up the wooden steps and across the wide porch of the feed store. Dismayed by his impulsive behavior and uncharacteristic loss of control, Nick got out of the van and followed her inside. In the wake of Erin's anger, he felt a little sheepish. He hadn't meant to offend her.

Lord knew *what* he'd meant. Nick, himself, wasn't entirely sure.

Erin was surprised when she became aware of him standing behind her at the counter. She'd half expected him to remain in the van. But then, on second thought, he didn't strike her as the type to pout. As she stared unseeing at the invoice the store clerk had given her to sign, she could still feel reaction to Nick's unexpected pass surging through her.

"Anything wrong?" the clerk asked when she remained motionless. "I told you our supplier hiked the prices, didn't I? Nothing we can do about it."

Erin blinked several times to clear her head. Nick's continued presence was doing nothing toward restoring her equilibrium. Reminding herself that she was offended and annoyed at him, and not the least bit intrigued, she quickly signed her name to the invoice.

"It's okay, Ben. I understand all about rising prices."

The younger man's frown of concern smoothed out immediately. "Good," he said. "Need a hand with these?" He indicated the two huge bags on the floor beside the counter.

"Thanks. I brought some muscle with me, too." Quickly, Erin introduced Nick, who reached past her to shake Ben's hand. "Nick's sister is one of our students, and he's helping Darren while they're here," she explained while Nick hefted one of the bags. She watched him take the weight as if it were nothing.

"Mind unlocking the back door for me?" he asked, glancing pointedly at the van keys she was holding.

"Of course." As Ben picked up the other bag, Erin rushed after Nick, who'd already started for the van, shouldering his way through the front door of the store before she could get to it.

Wordlessly, she opened the van and moved out of the way. She glanced at Nick's face, but his expression was unreadable. For a moment, Erin wondered what would have happened if she'd taken him up on his suggestion. She almost choked on her indrawn breath. Then sanity returned. Ben dumped the second bag next to the first, and Nick shut the door.

Raising his brows, he asked, "Anything else?"

"No, that's all." Erin thanked Ben, got behind the wheel and started the engine. Nick climbed in beside her. While he was still fastening his seat belt, she pulled away from the feed store. He'd certainly distracted her from her original intent, getting him to leave.

"In a hurry to go back?" he asked as she drove toward the highway.

Erin spared him a brief glance, congratulating herself for acting as cool as he was. "Yes, as a matter of fact, I am. Dinner's in a half hour and I'm hungry."

Nick fell silent, studying the passing countryside between Snohomish and Monroe, mostly pastureland and belts of trees. Briefly, he contemplated suggesting they stop somewhere in town to eat, but quickly discarded the idea. What he needed was to put some space between them. The silence in the van grew and Erin switched the radio on to a country station.

"We need to talk," Nick said over a male voice singing about old flames with new names.

"Talk about what?" Erin was curious, but she kept her attention on the road.

"About your idea that I go home." An idea he rejected out of hand.

Something in Nick's tone made her really look at him. "I didn't mean for you to take it personally," she began, then grimaced. Obviously, he took the whole thing very personally or he wouldn't have made the outrageous suggestion that she kiss him.

"It doesn't matter," Nick interrupted before she could go on. "I'm not leaving until Lucy does."

Somehow, his answer didn't surprise Erin. That would have been too easy. Maybe she was the one letting things get personal.

"I really think it would be easier if you weren't here to distract her."

He shifted in the bucket seat and ran a hand through his black hair, leaving it in careless disarray. The gesture was so casually sexy that Erin caught her breath. Then she clamped down ruthlessly on her growing attraction. This foolishness had to stop.

"I think I'm the best judge of what's good for my sister," Nick said as he caught her looking at him again. "Keep your eyes on the road!"

His sudden command made her jump. She'd only glanced at him

for the merest fraction of a second. "Don't tell me how to drive," she snapped back without thinking. Then she noticed that his hands were fisted on his knees, knuckles white, and his expression was rigid.

"I'm sorry." His voice was a rasp of pain.

"What is it?" Erin asked, filled with sudden compassion. "What's bothering you?"

Nick looked away, as if the view were utterly fascinating. "Nothing," he muttered. "Forget it. But I'm not leaving Monroe without my sister, so you might as well get used to having me around." He sounded as if he were meting out punishment.

Erin wondered if it was directed at her or himself. Several retorts danced on the tip of her tongue but she bit them back. "I'll have to talk to Lucy, then," she said instead. "See if I can get her to concentrate more in class."

"Just put the blame on me," Nick told her, and his tone was underscored with bitterness. "That's where it usually belongs, anyway."

Erin signalled and slowed the van to turn onto the road to the center. "I don't believe that," she said softly. "Anyone can see how much you care about Lucy. Perhaps you're being too hard on yourself."

He straightened and glared, his green eyes narrowed. "And perhaps you're making assumptions about things that don't concern you."

Erin stiffened, cheeks burning. "Sorry," she said, hurt. "It won't happen again."

She pulled to a stop by the supply room where the dog food was stored. Nick was out of the van and moving around back before she had her seat belt off. They were certainly getting good at rubbing each other the wrong way. She opened the door to the storage room and pointed, then watched wordlessly as he carried the bags, one at a time, and put them away. When he was done, he straightened.

"That all?"

She hesitated, but he'd made it plain that he wouldn't appreciate anything she had to say. "Yes. Thank you for your help. I guess I'll see you at dinner."

"Wait a minute." He glanced down at his feet.

Erin paused, curious. "What is it?"

He peered into the storage room as if he expected to find something there. "I, uh, think I owe you an apology," he muttered, again looking down.

Despite herself, Erin found some amusement in his obvious discomfort. It was a real contrast to his occasional displays of arrogance.

"Oh?" She had no intentions of helping him along. After all, he'd been way out of line and it wasn't as if he could read her mind and knew that she'd been speculating about him, too.

Speculating about his kisses.

She'd die if she thought he suspected.

"Yeah, I'm sorry about what I said earlier." He spoke quietly, finally meeting her gaze. "I've been worried about Lucy. When you said you wanted me to leave, I guess I just lost it. Went a little nuts."

"Are you saying a man would have to be crazy to kiss me?" she teased.

He looked dismayed. "No, of course not. I'm just trying to explain."

Suddenly Erin felt guilty for getting amusement out of his obvious concern. "Apology accepted," she said crisply. "Let's forget all about it."

"Good idea. Thanks for being so understanding." Some of his self-assurance was returning. As he heaved a sigh of relief, Erin could tell that he wasn't a man who was used to apologizing. The thought made her feel even more uncomfortable.

"I still think it would be best for Lucy if you went home," she insisted.

Instantly, the look of antagonism was back on Nick's face. "I don't agree. Lucy needs me here."

Erin shrugged, unwilling to argue further. "I'll see how she feels. For now, I'm hungry and I want some dinner."

"Good idea." Nick spun away without another glance.

Following him more slowly, Erin forced herself to think about Lucy and how best to approach the subject of her independence from Nick. Lucy wanted it, but did she have enough gumption to fight for it? Despite his determination that she keep relying on him. Erin suspected that his attitude toward Lucy was tied up with his guilt. Not that he'd ever see it that way, though.

For a moment, she pictured Nick's expression when he'd suggested that she kiss him. Had that been stark need she'd glimpsed in his eyes before he'd masked them with a gleam of humor? Reaction shivered through her at the thought of touching her lips to his. What if she had? Would the entire situation be more clear now, or hopelessly complicated? Pushing open the door to her apartment, Erin crossed to her bathroom to freshen up for dinner as her cat, Shiftless, greeted her with a glad meow. Somehow, she had to suspect that the latter, an unbearable complication, would have been true.

"I *am* trying. I pay attention and I do everything you ask us to. What haven't I done? Just tell me, okay?"

Erin sat in the chair in Lucy's unit and watched the other girl toss her head and gesture with her steadier hand, wondering how to make Lucy understand that she wasn't the enemy.

"See?" Lucy went on before Erin could speak. "There isn't one thing you can name that I haven't done, is there? Why are you hassling me, anyway? Is there something you don't like about me? Has my brother been giving you trouble? I'm not responsible—"

"No," Erin interrupted. "Nick has nothing to do with this." A little voice inside her asked if she was sure about that, but she ignored the taunt.

"Then I don't understand," Lucy said.

Before she could start another tirade, Erin got to her feet. "I'm trying to tell you," she said with exaggerated patience. "It's not anything you're doing wrong. It's just an instinct I have that you aren't entirely focused on the class, that there's something else going on with you."

Lucy shook her head emphatically as her dark hair fanned across her oval face. "No way," she said. "I'm here to get a dog. Period. Then Nick will see that I'm capable of running my life and managing on my own. Maybe he'll back off."

Erin was beginning to understand. "Do this for yourself, not just to show Nick," she said quietly as she put a hand on Lucy's shoulder.

There were tears in the other girl's hazel eyes when she looked up at Erin. "I am." Her tone had lost some of its certainty.

Erin smiled gently. "Just allow yourself to believe that you're worth it, that you deserve a dog." She squeezed Lucy's shoulder before dropping her hand. "Believe it," she repeated. "Because you *are* worth it."

For a moment Lucy was silent. "Okay," she said finally. "I guess you might be right. I was trying to prove something to Nick. But he holds on so tight. He doesn't want me to do anything on my own." A tear spilled over and ran down her cheek. Impatiently, she wiped it away. "Sometimes I feel like I can't breathe."

"Guilt can make a person act like Nick is doing," Erin ventured. She still wondered about the accident. Nick had told her that he was responsible for Lucy's injuries.

Lucy's eyes widened. "Guilt! Why would he feel guilty?"

It was Erin's turn to be surprised. "Because of the accident."

Lucy's face paled. "It wasn't his fault!" she cried. "A drunk driver ran a red light and hit my side of the car. The police said there was nothing Nick could have done." She set her jaw. "Why did you think it was his fault, anyway?"

Erin hadn't meant to upset Lucy, but now she was genuinely confused. "Nick told me it was," she said. "He said he was the one who'd put you in the chair."

For a moment, Lucy looked dazed. Then she whispered, "I didn't know he felt that way. He never told me." She focused her gaze on Erin. "Why would he say that? He can't think I blame him."

Erin wasn't sure what to say. Nick did blame himself. "I guess you'll have to ask him," she said, hoping she hadn't inadvertently opened up something that would only cause more pain. "Just don't do it tonight. It's getting late and we're going on a field trip tomorrow, so you need your rest. I'll send your attendant in to help you."

"Pretty soon I won't need an attendant," Lucy said, surprising Erin with her renewed confidence and enthusiasm. "Wait a minute, would you?" she asked as Erin pulled open the door.

She hesitated. Lucy looked so like Nick, but in a softer, more feminine way. She really was a beautiful girl. For an instant, Erin wondered what Lucy's plans had been before the accident changed her life. "What is it?"

Lucy's smile wavered. "I just wanted to say thanks," she admitted. "I'm glad you came by."

Erin returned her smile, relieved. "So am I. All I want is for you to succeed, you know. To have a happy life."

Lucy's head bobbed. "I know. And I'm glad to be here. Really. I'll think about what you said, and I'll try harder."

Erin wanted to urge her again to talk to her brother, but she'd said enough about that. "Would it make things easier for you if Nick left and went home?" she asked instead.

"That's what *Nick* was about to ask her," drawled a familiar voice.

Erin jerked her head around. Nick was standing in the open doorway, brows raised.

"Campaigning for my removal?" he asked lightly.

"Not at all." Erin went hot all over, as if she'd been caught red-handed even though she was perfectly innocent. "Lucy and I were discussing her progress in the course." She lapsed into silence, determined not to let him put her on the defensive. If Lucy wanted to tell him what they'd talked about, that was up to her.

Nick found himself studying Erin's face in the golden glow of the porch light. Lord, she was a lovely woman, and so passionate about everything. Hastily, he shut down the observance before it could expand into need.

"I'd like to talk to my sister," he said instead.

Annoyance flared in Erin's blue eyes and then her expression smoothed over. "Sure," she said in a deceptively bland tone. "But it's important that Lucy know how I feel." She turned to his sister, who was watching them anxiously. "Nick and I have already discussed this. He knows that I think you might be better off if he went back to Eugene."

Nick stepped forward before Lucy could reply. "And I disagree," he told Erin, ignoring the tightening of her lips. He took a deep breath, wondering how she would react to the risk he was about to take. "But I'll abide by Lucy's decision if you will."

Erin looked as if she would have liked to argue. Instead, she glanced at Lucy with an encouraging smile. "Okay. I'll leave you, then." Relief poured through Nick as she brushed past him.

"Thanks," he told her, surprised that she was giving him the opportunity to plead his case in private. Whenever he thought he had Erin pegged, she always danced away again, elusive as a ripple on the water. He watched the door close softly behind her and then braced himself.

"So?" he asked Lucy as he dropped into a straight-backed chair. "Has Erin persuaded you to give me the heave-ho?" His stomach clenched as he waited for his sister's reply. He'd had no intention of letting her decide his fate, but his confrontation with Erin had rattled him more than he'd realized.

"Well," Lucy said slowly, as if she relished the opportunity to leave him twisting on the spit, "I can get along without you, you know."

Nick's heart sank. He wanted desperately to stay. "You *think* you can get along without me," he couldn't keep from saying.

While he forced himself to watch her progress, Lucy rolled her chair away and then turned to face him. Before the accident, she'd talked about a modeling career, among other ideas. He'd taken her freedom to choose away from her. Now it was his duty to care for her. A life for a life. His freedom for hers. The idea shocked him—it was the first time he'd thought of it in quite that light.

"But how can I show you that I can get along without you if you aren't here to see me?" Lucy mused aloud, interrupting his line of thought.

Nick began to hope that she wasn't going to try to make him leave after all. "Good question."

Lucy returned his smile. "I want you to stay, brother dear. I want you to *see* how well I do with my dog."

He started to thank her but she cut him off. "And then," she said dramatically, "I want you to admit it."

"Admit what?" For a moment, Nick wished it could happen. Then reality returned.

"Admit that I can manage on my own, with my dog," Lucy insisted.

He rose before she could go on. He'd heard all he wanted, and it was getting late. No reason to discourage her. "I'll stay as long as you need me," he began, stopping when Lucy frowned. "So you can show me that you don't," he amended. If he remained at the center with her, she'd see how much she relied on him. No dog was going to change that.

While Nick talked to his sister, Erin had gone to the dining room to have a last cup of coffee. Lucy's attendant, an older woman who lived nearby, was sitting alone at the long table, sipping from a blue mug.

"Lucy ready for me?" she asked as Erin sat down across from her.

Erin glanced out the window to the other building. She saw Nick leave Lucy's unit and enter his own. "Yes, I think she is," she replied, resisting the urge to go back and ask Lucy just what she'd decided. Erin was getting too involved with the Blackwoods, allowing herself to get drawn deeper into their lives. Into Nick's life. However, knowing and doing something about it were two different things. Remaining objective was getting more difficult all the time.

"I'm staying," Nick told her at breakfast the next morning. "Lucy agrees. If you'd rather, I'll find a motel in town as originally planned." His expression was challenging, but Erin knew that a confrontation would benefit no one and would only upset Lucy.

"I'll stick with our bargain," she said, smearing jam on a piece of toast. She'd tried to do what she thought was best for Lucy. Despite her reservations, Nick wasn't leaving. Part of her was glad. "You don't need to find a motel room. But my rules about interference with the classes still apply."

Nick nodded. "Agreed."

Erin watched him while he took his seat next to Lucy, who was talking animatedly to Jane on her other side.

"Problems?" Anna asked Erin in an undertone as she and Darren set their trays on the table.

"What? No, of course not. I just hope that Nick knows what he's doing," Erin muttered before she took a sip of her orange juice. She was aware that Anna and Darren exchanged glances, but she ignored them. Then, as she bit into her toast, a loud crash turned all their heads. Someone had dropped a breakfast tray.

"Would you go with us to the mall in Everett tomorrow?"

Nick's brows rose at Erin's request. Earlier, she'd warned him off but the situation had changed. Now she ignored his complacent expression. If he thought she was making excuses to be in his company, he was dead wrong.

"We usually have two volunteers who go with us on field trips, but one of them's sick. I could use your help."

"Sure." When Erin spotted him, Nick had been coming back along one of the paved pathways that snaked into a sprawling wooded area behind the center. Now he stood before her, thumbs hooked into the belt loops of his jeans. Something about his casual, almost insolent pose, made her want to rile him, just to see his reaction. Everything else about him made her want to reach out and touch him. Instead, she said her thanks and was about to go by the office to see if Anna was still working.

"Don't run off." Nick touched her arm lightly, the contact making her skin tingle despite the protection of her denim jacket. The nights had turned chilly; darkness was rolling in earlier. Even now, the light was receding. There would be frost on the ground in the morning.

It was Erin's turn to give him an enigmatic look.

"What do you want me to do?" he asked. "I mean, during the field trip. So I don't get in the way."

Erin felt herself coloring at his oblique reference to her earlier remark. "You do whatever's needed," she replied, refusing to rise to his jibe. She realized that her answer was less than helpful. "The students will be trying to work with their dogs. They'll feel self-conscious and the dogs will be excited. People will stare, not unkindly but out of curiosity. The first time a class goes out, we can only expect the unexpected. You might not have to do anything more than give a little general assistance." She shrugged. "We'll have to watch and wait, okay?"

His wide shoulders relaxed slightly under his jacket. "Okay."

Erin expected him to say good night and walk away, but instead he remained where he was, looking down at her. In the fading light, she couldn't read the expression in his eyes clearly, but still a response, more than she wanted, churned up inside her. She knew it would be prudent to leave.

"Lucy's doing better in class," she said instead. When had Erin ever done the prudent thing?

Nick's expression mellowed. "I thought so, too. She and Max seem to get along well."

His comment surprised her, knowing how he felt about the dogs. Erin had made the permanent assignments that morning. "Yes, I think he's the best match for Lucy. That's important. Jane's more comfortable with another Lab and Queenie seems perfect for Fred."

"What if it doesn't work out so neatly?" he asked, obviously curious. "What if two candidates in a class want the same dog?"

Erin leaned back against the cyclone fence. She enjoyed talking to Nick. When they weren't arguing.

"A candidate doesn't always get his first choice, but so far no one's really complained. All the dogs are well-trained, and I think everyone's just grateful to get one."

"Where do the puppies come from?" he asked. "I haven't seen any around here." He turned to prop his forearms on the top of the fence next to her. "Do they all live closeby?"

She would have liked to move further away from him, away from his warmth and his scent, but didn't. Maybe she needed to somehow find the time to get out more, to date occasionally. Her hormonal level was obviously reaching the overload stage. The thought of Nick's startled reaction if she lunged at him now almost made her chuckle.

"We have puppy trainers who do the preliminary training. One of them, Caroline Burns, lives in Monroe. She's usually here quite a bit helping me work the older dogs when I have a class going, but her daughter just had a baby and Caroline's gone to stay with her."

Erin did her best not to get caught up in admiring the strength of Nick's profile, silhouetted against the last reflections of light in the western sky. She thought a moment. "Then there's a retired marine on Camano Island who's trained several puppies for me. The rest of the trainers live further away. In fact, I have a black Lab puppy flying in from Boise on Saturday evening."

"You've got a remarkable support group," Nick commented. He patted his pocket absently as if he were looking for a cigarette.

"Quit recently?" Erin asked.

Out of the corner of her eye, she saw his grin. "Six months ago, but it still hits me. You ever smoke?"

"Briefly, in college. I gave it up before quitting got too difficult."

"Good idea," Nick drawled, dropping his hand.

Erin looked up at the sky. Tomorrow would be clear and cold.

She wondered if he'd thought much about kissing her, before he'd suggested it. Or since. Her cheeks warmed. What if he could somehow tell what she was thinking? "Have you got more family back in Oregon?" she asked, to distract them both. She was reluctant to break off the conversation totally when they seemed to be getting along so well.

"Just parents." He gazed into the distance thoughtfully. "My father worked construction, finally started up on his own. He did good work, was lucky, too, I guess. He got some big jobs and the business grew. When I took over, we kept expanding."

"What kind of projects do you build?" she asked, to keep him talking.

"Mostly big commercial jobs now. Some mini-malls, office buildings, discount stores."

A sudden breeze came up, making Erin shiver.

Nick was instantly concerned. "You're getting cold."

She shook her head. "Not really. I like the change of seasons."

Nick picked up the thread of their conversation. Maybe he, too, was enjoying the truce between them. "Dad keeps a hand in the business, but they like to travel, so I take care of the day-to-day details."

He made it sound so unimportant. "Who's minding the store while you're gone?" she asked, wondering how he could be away for a whole month.

"My parents are just home from Greece. It's the first long trip they've taken since—" his voice stumbled, "—since the accident."

"I'm sorry," Erin said, straightening. "I didn't mean to bring up bad memories."

He shook his head. "You didn't. The memory's always with me, anyway. It's not something that goes away."

Erin searched for something else to say. "Tomorrow night the dogs start sleeping in the units with the students. They've gotten used to that as puppies and none of them really like the kennels, anyway. We'll cut back on the attendants and in another week we'll hardly need them. I think you'll notice a real bonding take place very shortly."

"You trying to convince me that Lucy won't need me anymore?" he asked lightly.

Erin made her voice even. "I don't think you're needed in quite the way you think right now," she said.

Nick was silent for so long she thought he didn't intend to speak again. Finally he shifted so that he faced her. "Maybe you're right." He didn't sound convinced. "I've enjoyed talking to you," he admitted. "And I can think of better ways to end the evening than by arguing."

Erin told herself he must mean something other than the possibility that leapt to her obviously R-rated mind. While she was wondering, Nick straightened. She watched him cautiously. As he continued to study her, his teasing expression went abruptly serious.

For a giddy moment, Erin wondered if he really could read her mind. While she debated what to say to defuse the suddenly tense situation, he thrust a hand beneath her chin and tipped her head back. Her hungry gaze locked on his as she felt his breath against her lips.

Nick's voice was a soft, predatory growl. "If I kiss you now, will I end up apologizing again?" he whispered.

Four

Part of Erin wished that Nick hadn't asked permission, that he had just lowered his head and taken the kiss she wanted so badly to give him. The rest of her, no doubt the more sensible part, was relieved that he hadn't.

"That's probably not such a good idea," she said breathlessly as she retreated a step.

His fingers released her chin and his hand dropped to his side. "I suppose not," he agreed.

Erin did her best to ignore the disappointment that shivered through her at his capitulation.

"Well, I guess I'll see you at breakfast." There wasn't anything else left to say. "Good night."

" 'Night." If he had any regrets, he hid them well.

Erin turned and walked determinedly to her apartment, no longer in the mood to spend time in the office. She thought she could feel Nick's gaze on her back, then decided she was being fanciful. The temptation to turn around and see was strong but she resisted.

When she opened her apartment door, Shiftless jumped down
from the couch and padded over to butt his head against her leg.

"Hello, baby." Murmuring a greeting, Erin bent down to stroke
the cat's soft fur. He meowed again but she ignored him, walking
into the small, spotless kitchen of her unit and glancing around
restlessly. Usually her apartment was a refuge from responsibility
and worry, but tonight it felt more like a prison.

Erin had a sharp craving for something sweet, preferably something chocolate. She slid open a drawer. Empty. Looked into a
cupboard. Nothing. She tapped her fingers on the counter, decided
she didn't need a chocolate fix bad enough to drive to the store.
Opened another cupboard and stared at its contents without seeing
a thing.

She thought about Nick and frowned. Why had he decided to
stay at the center, to distract her with his dark, brooding attraction?

"I can handle him," she told Shiftless, who had abandoned his
own quest for a treat and settled again onto the couch. Even the
cat's expression bordered on disbelief. "I can," she muttered again,
emptying a half dozen chocolate chips from a bag she had found
crumpled in the back of another drawer. For Lucy's sake as well
as her own, she had to ignore the attraction churning inside her.

Letting the last of the chips melt on her tongue, she crumpled
the empty bag and tossed it into the trash under the sink.

Too bad all cravings weren't as simple to appease.

The field trip went no better or worse than Erin had expected.
First outings with a new group always brought with them a few
surprises. She, Nick and Ray, the other volunteer, were all wearing
orange windbreakers with "NW Companion Dogs" silkscreened
on the backs in navy blue lettering. The dogs wore their orange
harnesses.

As soon as the group made their way into the covered mall,
Queenie got loose and trotted over to a baby in a stroller, tail wagging.

"Call her back," Erin told Fred, who was sitting in his chair
silently.

"Queenie, come," he shouted. She returned willingly enough.
"My lap," Fred said, and she put her forepaws up on his spindly

thighs. Her tail wagged furiously. He laughed and patted her head. "Kiss," he demanded. Queenie gave his chin a lick.

"Now have her sit," Erin instructed.

Fred did so, his grin wide. Queenie obeyed promptly. Erin was happy to see how well they worked together.

A few moments later, a clerk in one of the stores the group visited tried to evict Max, but quickly relented when Erin explained that service dogs were exempted from the health department ordinance against bringing dogs into retail establishments.

"Anything I can do to help?" the clerk asked anxiously as Lucy wheeled her chair toward a display of washable silk blouses. The woman reached down to pat Max, whose full golden tail began to wave in friendly response.

"Remind Max that he's working," Erin told Lucy in a low voice.

Lucy gave the commands to heel and lie down. Max obeyed promptly, eyes on his mistress.

"The dogs can't allow themselves to be distracted when they're working," Erin explained to the clerk, pointing to the distinct harness with curved handle and attached saddlebags. "Anytime they're wearing this. We don't want them to miss something important."

"I'm sorry," the clerk said quickly. "I didn't mean to get the dog in trouble."

Lucy patted Max's wide head. "No problem," she said with a smile. "Max and I are still learning to work together." She returned her attention to the rack of blouses.

Erin glanced up when Nick came toward them. Before she could speak, the clerk, an attractive blonde, approached him.

"May I help you?" she asked, her voice warming several degrees.

A sudden impulse to warn the clerk off had Erin moving forward without thinking. She almost told the other woman that Nick was with them and didn't need help. The possessive instinct dismayed her and she turned deliberately away, biting her lip as she left Nick to keep an eye on his sister.

Erin walked quickly out into the covered mall area, looking for Ray, the postal clerk who often accompanied them on field trips. He was with Fred, Jane and their dogs outside a music store.

"How's it going?" Erin asked.

"Great!" Fred burst out. Queenie waited at his side, alert for his next command. "I want to go to the toy store."

Erin glanced at Ray. "Go ahead," she said. "Meet us at the book-store. I'll stay with Jane."

Ray nodded and trailed after Fred and Queenie, who was pulling the chair as Fred held onto the handle of her harness with one hand and her leash with the other.

"I sure missed getting out like this," Jane said, absently stroking Ranger's black head. The dog cast her an adoring glance. "Having someone take me wasn't the same as being with Dottie."

Erin nodded, understanding what Jane meant. She was pleased to see that the bond so necessary between human and animal was already forming between this pair.

"We won't do much today," she told Jane. "You've been through this before, but it will be tiring to the others."

"I remember," Jane said as she watched the groups of shoppers walk by. Most of them ignored her as she sat in her chrome chair. A little girl stared curiously and her mother pulled her away, whis-pering earnestly in her ear.

Erin wished the other shoppers would treat her charges like real people instead of a life form to be ignored or pitied. While she was thinking that, an older man with white hair slowed and smiled at Jane.

"That's a beautiful dog," he said.

"Thank you." Jane's answering smile brightened her face as the man walked on.

"Go on ahead to the bookstore, if you want," Erin told her. "I'll be right along." Jane rolled away, Ranger at her side.

Erin was just about to go back and look for Lucy, Max and Nick when she saw them emerge from another clothing store. Lucy was carrying a shopping bag across her knees.

"Nick bought me a blouse," she said, as soon as they were within hearing distance. Max trotted along next to her.

Erin moved closer. "This isn't a shopping trip," she told Lucy sharply. "You're here to practice with your companion."

Nick's chin went up. "She saw a blouse she wanted. No harm done." His narrowed eyes held a challenge Erin didn't intend to take up in the middle of the mall.

"It's almost time to leave," she said instead. "Lucy, why don't you and Max go on ahead. You know what to do. We'll meet you in front of the bookstore, okay?" She pointed down the wide mall aisle. "Right over there."

Lucy glanced from Erin to Nick and back again, a frown marring her smooth forehead. "Sure." Beside the chair, Max sat watching her intently. "Max, heel." He rose immediately.

Erin's pace was deliberately slow. As Nick fell in beside her, he sighed and jammed his hands into the pockets of his orange jacket.

"Okay," he said. "I can feel you gearing up for a scold. What did I do wrong this time?"

"Nothing," Erin said, trying to be fair. She hadn't told him not to buy anything, had only assumed he'd know to watch Lucy without interfering. "I just get a little nervous during the first outing with a class. Sorry."

Erin glanced around at Nick, who had come to a halt while other shoppers filed around him.

"Come on," she urged him. "We have to meet the others. It's time to go back to the center."

"Sure, no problem." He shrugged, shoulders broad beneath the bright orange jacket, but at least he started moving again.

"Is this the kind of place your company builds?" Erin asked to distract him.

Nick grinned, as if he knew what she was up to. He glanced around at the high, arched ceiling as they strolled through an intersection in the mall. A shallow pool surrounded by green plants and plastic chairs formed an island of sorts in the wide expanse of tiled flooring.

"Yeah," he said after a moment. "Among other things. Of course, we do a much better job than this. Skylights, comfortable seating areas, more visual interest."

"Of course," Erin agreed. She could see the others waiting in front of the bookstore. Next to Fred, Queenie watched a little boy, barely old enough to walk, toddle toward them. The dog reached out her nose to sniff him as Fred said something to her. Immediately, she straightened.

"Good for you," Erin told Fred with an apologetic glance at the little boy's mother. "It's important to remind Queenie why she's here."

"We're practicing," Erin explained to the woman, who had paused by Fred's chair.

"My brother has a companion dog." She scooped up her small son. "It's changed his life."

"That's good to hear," Erin told her. "Thank you." She glanced at Ray. "All set?"

He nodded in return. "It went well today. No disasters."

Erin returned his grin, knowing he was thinking of other trips and some of the things that had happened. A dog that couldn't "hold it," a little girl in tears when she became self-conscious and forgot the commands, and a young man who was so busy watching a group of teenage girls that he ran into a clearance table despite his dog's efforts to steer him past it. Yes, in comparison today's outing had gone well.

"You all did very nicely," Erin said, looking around at the group before her. "We'll come here again before graduation." With an inadvertent glance at Nick, who was watching her with a thoughtful expression, she turned to lead them back to the vans.

Nick was relieved when the trip was over. If he had been forced to keep watching Erin in her snug powder blue jeans and the bright orange jacket that should have clashed with her hair and somehow didn't, he might have blown a gasket. When they had been walking together after the others, he almost reached for her hand. Wouldn't that have been embarrassing? Especially after she chastised him for buying Lucy that damned blouse.

He thought Erin was too uptight and needed to lighten up, but she still attracted him on a gut level he was having trouble ignoring. But had to continue to ignore the best he could.

Erin was the last person for him to get involved with, no matter how temporarily. He had Lucy to think about, and that left no time for a romantic tryst. Just as his sister's life had changed when the drunken driver hit Nick's car, so had his. Irrevocably.

"I'm pleased with today's field trip," Erin told her charges at the end of class that day.

Nick watched Lucy's smile widen to the grin he remembered so well when Fred turned and said something Nick couldn't understand. Lucy nodded to the younger boy and bent to pat Max's head.

"Can't we keep the dogs with us tonight?" she asked Erin in the pleading tone Nick always found so hard to resist.

Erin only laughed and shook her head. "Soon," she said. "But for now, let's go over the material for tomorrow morning's quiz so we can break for dinner. Are you all clear on which commands you need to learn?"

Nick knew they had a test at the start of class each morning to review what they had covered the day before. Lucy studied every night, sometimes enlisting his aid in drilling her on the answers.

After dinner that evening, a lively affair spent going over and over every minute of their first field trip, Nick took a solitary walk along one of the paved paths and then wandered back to Lucy's unit. He had thought of a couple questions he could ask Erin, giving him the excuse to seek her out, then sworn under his breath when he realized what he'd been doing.

Erin was off limits. Why did he seem to have so much trouble remembering that?

Muttering another curse, he knocked on Lucy's door. "It's me, Nick," he shouted. Automatically, he reached to open the door and then remembered her earlier admonition that he let her answer it. She needed the practice, she said.

To his surprise, instead of seeing the door open before him, he heard a muffled shout.

"Nick. Nick! Help me."

He practically tore the door off its hinges when he wrenched it open. Lucy lay on the carpet, her chair on its side.

Nick froze at the sight, his heart leaping to his throat and lodging there.

"Oh, Peanut, are you okay?" He dropped to one knee beside her, his hand shaking as he extended it toward her. Vivid images of Lucy as she looked right after the accident, pale and covered with blood, her eyes shut, flashed before him as he grabbed her hand.

Her cheeks were wet with tears but she managed a tiny smile.

"I'm okay. I just feel like an idiot." She tugged on his hand. "Help me up. I should be able to get back in my chair by myself but I just couldn't manage."

Nick's worry turned to churning anger, spilling out as he grabbed her beneath the arms and lifted her back into the conveyance he had righted.

"Are you sure you aren't hurt? Maybe I should call a doctor." Concern made his voice harsh.

"I'm okay," she insisted. "I just tipped over."

"This is exactly why I don't want you left alone," he burst out as she wheeled the chair around to face him. "What if I hadn't come along?"

Lucy shrugged casually, but her cheeks were flushed. "Someone would have found me eventually."

Nick whirled away from her and braced the flats of his hands against the wall, bowing his head and sucking in a deep breath. "That's not good enough!" He thought about counting to ten, got to three and abandoned the effort.

"You could have been badly hurt," he ground out, voice escalating. "In serious danger. A fire—"

"Nick! There was no fire." She rolled her eyes.

"But there could have been," he continued insistently. "You would have been trapped. Maybe you don't want to admit it, but you need me around. Either me or a paid attendant."

Lucy sighed and began to nibble her lower lip. "I have to study," she said without meeting his gaze. "Thanks for rescuing me, okay?"

Nick knew a dismissal when he heard one. Okay. He had a few choice things to say to Erin McKenzie, anyway. God, his hands were still shaking and his gut was in knots.

"Yeah, sure she's fine now, but she could have been hurt. What if I hadn't got there when I did?"

Erin watched Nick pace back and forth in front of her desk like a sleek black panther on the prowl. She'd been going over a few letters that Anna had left for her signature when he'd burst in, flames all but crackling in his green eyes. At first she thought that Lucy had been hurt; it had taken a moment to sort out that she hadn't.

"I'm glad your sister's okay," Erin repeated, hoping to calm him. "These things happen. People in chairs do fall." She was trying her best to hang onto her patience, but Nick was testing it severely, refusing to listen, going on and on about what could have occurred but in all likelihood never would. Especially after Lucy got her dog.

"Not my sister," he ground out, stopping to stare down at Erin intently. "These things don't happen to her."

More affected by his appearance that she would have admitted, Erin pushed back her chair and stood so she didn't have to look up quite so far to see his face.

"And they won't again," she said in an overly sweet tone. "When Max is with Lucy at night, he'll take care of her if she should fall out of her chair and not be able to get back in."

Nick's expression bordered on disbelief. "How is the dog going to help? Is he trained to call 911? Or will he grab her sleeve with his teeth and drag her back into the chair?"

Erin ignored his thinly-veiled sarcasm. "Neither. He's trained to lick her cheek and see if she responds. If she doesn't, he'll go for help, barking and scratching at doors until he finds someone."

Nick's expression had softened from skepticism to reluctant interest. "Then what?" His voice was gruff. He reminded Erin of a stubborn child, unwilling to give in to his curiosity.

"He'll whine and take their hand gently in his mouth, tugging on it until they go with him. Anyone who knows there's a handicapped person in the vicinity would follow."

Nick seemed to ponder her words. "He can't call for an aid car, though."

"No," Erin agreed. "We haven't figured out how to teach the companion dogs that trick yet."

His smile was wry. "Okay," he said reluctantly. "I can see where a dog might be some help."

Erin snorted at his continued skepticism, but inside she was surprised at his grudging concession. Was she supposed to be grateful?

"Well, I'm glad to see that you're beginning to recognize the dogs' value," she said, knowing he was still far from accepting any such thing. "I'll go over and check on Lucy as soon as I've signed these letters."

"What are they?" Nick asked, glancing at the top of her littered desk. "Pleas for donations?"

Erin was tempted to let him think what he liked. "No," she replied finally. "They're answers to requests for dogs. Turndowns, I'm afraid. Because we don't have the funds to train anywhere near the number of companion animals to meet the demand." She rubbed at her forehead where a headache was forming. "It's difficult choosing who gets a dog and who doesn't."

For once she saw honest understanding and even sympathy on his roughly handsome face.

"I bet it's hard to say no."

Erin blinked back a sudden rush of moisture. "Damn hard."

"The plane's coming in late and I hate to go down there by myself at night," Erin found herself explaining to Nick awkwardly. "And I hate to take Darren away from Anna on a Saturday evening. They don't have much leisure time together as it is." She had to pick up the puppy from Boise at the airport and the cargo area could be intimidating at that time of night.

"We could stop to eat on the way," she continued. "My treat." As a bribe, it wasn't much, but Nick might be getting tired of hanging around the center.

His hooded eyes studied her for a moment, and then he straightened from the fence surrounding the kennels that he'd been leaning against. "Sure. Why not. I'll just check on Lucy first, okay?"

The tension in Erin melted with relief. She had just about decided that asking him had been a major mistake. "Yeah. We don't have to leave for about an hour. Last I saw Lucy, she was in the rec room playing a game with Freddie."

"Where shall I meet you?" Nick asked.

"By the van?"

He nodded. "Okay, see you in about an hour."

"Nick?" she called as he turned away. He looked over his shoulder.

"Thanks."

His brows drew into a frown. "Sure." Then he was gone. Erin stroked the nose of one of the dogs who poked his muzzle through a gap in the cyclone fencing.

"I guess I'll never figure him out," she muttered. Her forlorn tone made her glance around guiltily, relieved that no one but the dogs had heard her. The question that popped into her head, and that she studiously ignored as she cleaned the pens, was why she even bothered trying.

* * *

Erin and Nick stopped for hamburgers at a fast-food chain with inside seating. Nick insisted on paying and, after a brief argument, Erin gave in.

"Thanks again," she said, as she bit into an onion ring. "I'd almost forgotten that a bacon burger and a milk shake can be satisfying on a deeper level than just hunger."

Nick's grin was light-hearted compared to his habitual thoughtful frown. "Soul food to a whole generation," he said, as he popped a hand-cut french fry into his mouth. "Food like this brings back memories of high school and happier times."

Erin chewed thoughtfully. "I don't know about happier," she admitted. "Maybe more carefree in a way, less filled with responsibility."

"Did you date a lot in high school?" Nick asked as he picked up his hamburger. He took a huge bite without waiting for her reply.

"I had a boyfriend for a couple of years," she admitted. She hadn't thought of Ned in ages. Wondered now what he was doing. He'd been fun and, for a while, they had been torridly in love. But they had both outgrown the feeling and parted friends.

"Mmm," Nick muttered as he chewed and swallowed. "A one-man woman."

Erin laughed. "Not intentionally. I just wasn't that popular. Except for Ned and a few random dates, I ran around with a couple of girlfriends most of the time."

"Ned?" Nick's brows rose. "Kind of a nerdy name if you ask me."

Erin threw a small onion ring at him. It bounced off his chest and landed on the table between them. He tossed it into his mouth. "Thanks. Want a fry?" He picked up a long, skinny one and tossed it back at her. Erin caught it in her hand and dipped it in the small pool of ketchup she had squeezed onto the foil wrapping paper in front of her.

"Yum. Great greasy food. And Ned wasn't a nerd. He was sweet."

Nick made a gagging sound, selected another fry and dipped it in her ketchup. Then, eyes gleaming, he held it out to her. Their gazes clashed briefly before she opened her mouth. Carefully, he

fed her the french fry. When she held out another onion ring, he
bit into it, showing his teeth. With the second bite he managed to
touch her fingers with his tongue.

Erin pulled back, a funny feeling zigzagging up her arm.
Nick looked smug. Determined not to reveal the extent of her
reaction to the unexpected caress, she held out another onion
ring. Surprise lit his eyes. Then he grinned and lunged forward, gobbling the ring and nuzzling her fingers as she
shrieked with surprise.

Heat bathed Erin's cheeks as she glanced around at the other
patrons, several of whom were looking their way with indulgent
expressions.

"I think we'd better get going," she said hastily, rising.

"Surely I have time to finish my coffee." Nick picked up the
heavy white china cup while she sank back down, more embarrassed than ever.

"I don't want the puppy waiting any longer than necessary," she
muttered belligerently. "She'll be frightened enough by the crate
and the airplane ride."

"Where's she coming from, Boise?" Nick asked as he sipped
his coffee.

"Yup."

Finally Nick drained his cup and rose. "Let's go."

Feeling as if she were the one who had been holding them up,
Erin went out the door he held open for her.

"Tell me about this puppy," Nick said when they were headed
back down the interstate on their way to the airport.

"She's a black Lab named Lulu. The second one we've gotten
from this trainer. The first one turned out to be an excellent companion and I have high hopes for Lulu, also."

"She still needs more training, right?" Nick asked as he signalled
and changed lanes to avoid a slow-moving lumber truck.

"About six more months," Erin answered, content to study his
profile. He drove as he did everything else, with quiet strength and
assurance. "We'll do that right at the center."

"How do you find the time?"

Erin hesitated. Should she tell him that she had no social life,
almost no personal life to speak of? No, she didn't want him to
pity her, only wished he would understand just a little how long

and hard she had worked to get the center going, to keep it running in the black.

"Caroline usually helps me," she reminded him. "She's wonderful with the dogs, especially the new puppies."

Nick glanced at her before turning his attention back to the thickening traffic. "New puppies?"

"Well, actually, they're over a year old when we get them. Like the one we're picking up tonight." Erin always found that getting the new dogs was exciting. There was so much to learn about them. If they had been well-trained. If they were intelligent and had the right temperament for service work.

Beside her, Nick drove silently. "Do you miss Eugene?" she asked, to get him talking again. She wondered if he had a girlfriend back home. Maybe even more than one. A man as handsome as Nick, as successful, would surely have women friends. Erin was surprised that he wasn't married. Maybe there had been someone, before Lucy's accident if not now.

"Yeah, I miss home," he chuckled, signalling and taking the exit that would eventually lead them to the airport. "I miss my dog."

It was the last thing that Erin had expected him to say. The meaning of his words even took a moment to sink in.

"Your dog?" she echoed. She hadn't pictured him with a dog. "What kind?"

"Bassett Hound. His name is Sparky and Lucy says I've spoiled him rotten."

"That doesn't surprise me," Erin replied softly as they passed the sign directing them to the cargo pickup area. "I bet you'd spoil Lucy, too, if she'd let you."

Nick's gaze had narrowed when he glanced her way. "I don't want to spoil Lucy," he argued. "All I want is to take care of her. The way she deserves. A dog, no matter how well he's been trained, can't do that."

Erin had thought they'd made some progress. Obviously, she was mistaken. Disappointed, she sat back in her seat and watched as Nick drove toward the building she had indicated.

"You're so wrong about the dogs and about Lucy," she murmured as he parked the van. "I guess I'll just have to see if I can change your mind about that."

"You can't," he said after they had both climbed out and stood facing each other. "As soon as both you and Lucy finally accept that, we'll all be better off."

Five

By the time Erin had claimed the crate with Lulu inside and taken care of all the necessary paperwork, the puppy was whining frantically. Her brown-eyed stare was intent and her pink tongue kept licking at the mesh of her carrier.

"I think I know what she needs," Erin said, glancing around the parking lot as Nick carried the crate to the van. "Set her down on the ground, would you."

Nick complied and she took a leash from the pocket of her windbreaker. Kneeling, she swung open the door and snapped the lead to Lulu's collar. Lulu licked her hand and danced around excitedly as Erin straightened.

"Good girl. I'll bet you're glad to be off the airplane, huh?"

Lulu yipped in reply.

"Okay," Erin said in a soothing voice. "Lulu, heel."

The dog's ears went up and she obeyed instantly, prancing along beside Erin as she led her to a landscaped island of bark and shrubs in the middle of the sea of concrete. As soon as Lulu had found a spot and answered nature's call, Erin took her back to the carrier. The puppy, wearing her canvas coat with the words "Service Dog in Training" stenciled on it, went docilely back inside. Erin took a minute to pet and reassure her before she shut the door and opened the back of the van.

"Put her in facing front, so she can see us, okay."

Nick did as Erin asked without speaking. It took an effort not to touch her, just to see if she felt as good, as warm and soft, as she looked. When they were on the road again, heading back to the center, he could feel her presence beside him even when he wasn't darting glances at her profile. He remembered the way her eyes had lit up when they teased each other back at the restaurant. He had wanted to reach across the table and stroke her face with his fingers. To lick the dot of ketchup from the side of her mouth.

To bury his fingers in her fiery hair and taste the salt on her full lips.

What he should have done, instead, was to warn her that she was playing with fire, that he was a man long deprived of feminine companionship except for that of his sister. That Erin's innocent flirting was fueling a conflagration in his gut that his body ached to put out in the time-honored way. Wouldn't she have been shocked if he had said any of those things? Confessed to the want that grew like a weed, unwanted and uncultivated. She would undoubtedly have considered him some kind of pervert who overreacted to a little innocent teasing.

Maybe he was. He sure as hell overreacted to her. Even now, having her sitting next to him was driving him crazy. Her scent, that mixture of flowers and soap and womanly warmth that surrounded her like an aura, seeped into his very pores. Made his mouth go dry and his fingers itch.

Nick swallowed. The puppy whined and Erin turned to speak to her.

"It's okay, Lulu. We'll be home soon."

The sound of her name apparently reassured the dog, who lay back down with a noisy sigh. Nick found the throaty tone of Erin's voice anything but soothing.

"Lulu doing okay?" he asked.

He could have sworn he felt it when Erin turned her attention on him. "Sure. She's used to riding in a car. I suppose I could have let her loose but you never know. A long trip, strange surroundings . . ." Her voice trailed off. "I like to work with them first, to see how much training they've really absorbed. The freeway can be so busy, and you never know what the crazy driver in the other car is about to do."

"True." Nick's tone was dry. "How well I know."

"Oh," Erin gasped. "I'm sorry. Of course you know."

He took one hand off the wheel and placed it on her arm. "Don't worry about it."

Beside him, she remained silent, and he cursed himself for making her feel awkward. He glanced at her and forced a grin. "Don't like the idea of a dog bouncing all over the inside of the van while I'm changing lanes, tuning in the radio and flirting with you, all at the same time?" he teased.

Her flashing grin was a reward that slammed into his gut, making him even more aware of her. Talk about a slavering sex-crazed hulk, he thought disparagingly, tightening his hands on the wheel. Maybe it was time he went home and accepted the none-too-subtle offer of the next woman who eyed him with ill-disguised interest, like Lucy was always telling him he should do.

As he rejected the idea out of hand, Erin reached forward. "You don't mind, do you?" she asked as she turned on the radio.

"No, of course not," Nick replied. "As long as it's not heavy metal or grunge music."

The song that drifted softly into the interior of the van was a current hit by one of his favorite artists.

"You like country?" he asked.

"Unless you hate it," she said quickly. "I can tune in something else."

He shook his head. "This is fine. It's what I listen to at home."

She seemed pleased by his answer, but didn't comment. Instead, they listened in companionable silence for several miles. Then Erin turned to check on Lulu again.

"We should be home in a little over a half hour," she muttered, mostly to herself, as she turned back and glanced around.

"Good." Nick flexed his shoulders and leaned forward to stretch his back. Perhaps confinement with him in the van was bothering her, too.

"I should have offered to drive home," Erin added, looking guilty when he rotated one shoulder. "I didn't think."

"I like driving," Nick replied. "Don't worry about it." Riding next to her without even that to distract him would have been infinitely worse.

With a small smile of relief, she leaned back and closed her eyes. Nick wondered how often she got a few moments to relax. From what he'd seen of her schedule, not often at all. She seemed to be on call twenty-four hours of the day at the center.

"What do you do when you aren't working?" he asked, hating to disturb her but too curious to save the question for another time.

Her eyes remained closed. "I like to go to my folks' house on Camano Island," she said. "It's right near the beach. I love to take long walks and watch the birds." She fell silent. "Other than that, most of my time goes to the center. I like it that way."

Her reply didn't surprise him. "Surely you need to get away sometimes," he said. "Anyone would. And it must be draining—the dogs, the clients and everyone's needs. Don't you ever get discouraged?"

Now her eyes opened and she did look at him. "No. Not really. Quite the opposite. It's uplifting, seeing people meet challenges and overcome them." She glanced away. "I guess what's tiring is the constant pursuit of funding. The presentations, the currying of corporate accounts for the kind of regular donations we can depend on." She sighed. "I know it's all necessary, but most of the time I'd rather be working with the dogs or running a class like the one that's going on now."

Nick thought of the paperwork that kept him trapped in the office when he would rather be out on a construction site. "I can understand that," he said. "Tell me more about corporate funding."

Until they turned into the driveway to the center, Erin did, explaining the different ways she raised money, about the field trips to schools and businesses, the slide shows, the talks she gave and the mailings Anna sent out.

Then she glanced around at their surroundings. "Sorry," she said contritely. "I didn't mean to bend your ear all the way home."

"You didn't." Nick parked the van and shut off the motor. "It was interesting. Really."

She rolled her eyes and grabbed the door handle. "I'm sure. Anyway, thanks for going with me. Now I'd better get Lulu out and settled in her kennel for the night. She'll hate it, after sleeping in her puppy trainer's bedroom all this time. I'm always tempted to let them sleep with me, at least the first night."

"Why don't you?" Nick's expression was unreadable.

"Because then I'd be facing the same dilemma the second night," she said. "It's easier in the long run to get it over with right away." More than anything, Erin knew she needed to get away from Nick's presence, from the dark, compelling attraction he held for her. She kept from bolting, but barely. Dragging in a lungful of the crisp, clear air, she made herself walk slowly to the back of the van.

Nick had beaten her there. He opened the door and stepped back, his green eyes on her.

"Are you going to let her out or do you want me to—"

"Oh, I'm sure our Lulu is more than ready to escape her cage,"

Erin said, opening the door. She had to calm her own nerves or Lulu would sense her tension.

For a moment, the dog merely sat and stared as if she couldn't quite believe that she was free.

"Come on, girl," Erin coaxed. "Time to look around your new home."

With a woof of pure joy, Lulu bounded out of the carrier and hopped down onto the ground. There she stood looking up at Erin, her whole body wiggling and her heavy tail swishing back and forth.

Then, when Erin gave her permission, she put her nose down and sniffed her way to a pink dogwood tree whose leaves had turned an intense red. While Lulu explored, Erin kept a close eye on her. Nick lifted the carrier out of the van and took it to the kennel area. Finally, Erin called to Lulu, who obeyed instantly.

As soon as the puppy was settled into a run and had made friends with her neighbors on either side, Erin redirected her attention to Nick, who stood watching the animals through the chain-link fence.

"Thanks again for your help. And for dinner." If it sounded like a dismissal, that was just too bad. She needed space, time to think and to regroup. He was far too attractive and she was dangerously smitten.

"Sure. I enjoyed it." He didn't glance at her, just kept watching Lulu. Around them, the night air was chilly. The collar of his jacket was turned up against the wind. "Think she'll be okay?"

"I'll check on her again before I go to bed." Since Nick still made no move to leave, she forced herself to turn away. Her hands and ears were getting cold. "See you," she called over her shoulder.

Her quick exit caught Nick by surprise. He had figured she might stick around to check on the other dogs, to talk about Lulu some more or Monday's training schedule. He realized he hadn't been ready to say good night. Now he watched her walk away until she turned the corner and disappeared behind a building.

Nick glanced up at the sky, solid black without a star showing, as he whistled tunelessly between his teeth. The air felt damp; maybe the clouds overhead were full of rain. He scratched idly at his jaw. Might as well check on Lucy. The next day was Sunday and there were no classes, but Darren would drive one of the vans to church in case anyone besides he and Anna wanted to go. After that, everyone's time was their own. Maybe Nick would see if his sister wanted to drive into Everett and have lunch, see a movie. He needed to get away from the center, to breathe in some air that didn't carry Erin's scent.

Lucy wasn't in her apartment. He found her in the cafeteria, playing cards with her attendant and the cook.

"Want a piece of pie?" Lucy asked when he walked in. "It's peach and there was some left over from dinner."

Nick nodded to the other two women as he grabbed a cup and poured himself some coffee. "No, thanks. We ate on the way to the airport."

"How's the new puppy doing?" Lucy asked.

He took a sip. "Seems fine." He was still restless. After turning down Lucy's offer to deal him in and watching several hands of an unfamiliar version of rummy played for toothpicks, he drained his cup and rose. Lucy was okay for now but he couldn't help remembering how she had looked when he found her sprawled on the floor of her unit. It was difficult not to mention it and caution her to be more careful. He felt as if everything in his life was moving beyond his control.

"Where are you off to?" Lucy asked after he had rinsed out his cup and left it next to the sink in the kitchen.

He shrugged. "I think I'll take a walk. You be okay?" If she asked, he would stay.

"I'm fine." Her grin was sassy. "I guess I'll see you in the morning, then."

"Guess so," he echoed, waving as he pushed through the door. Behind him, the three women resumed their game.

Halfway to Erin's apartment, he realized where he was headed. His feet slowed for a moment and then he bowed to the inevitable, knocking on her door before he could change his mind. Perhaps she was elsewhere, in the office or talking to Anna or back at the dog runs. He was already turning away when the door opened.

She wore a pale pink robe and her short, red hair was damp from a shower. She looked tired. While he tried to think of something to say, a water droplet ran down her neck and disappeared into the deep vee of the robe. He wondered if she was wearing anything under it.

"Hi." She mopped at her hair with a hand towel. "Something wrong?"

Yeah, he thought. But you don't want to know.

"I just wondered if you'd checked on Lulu again yet." The excuse sounded lame, even to him.

Apparently Erin didn't see anything odd about his comment. She opened the door wider.

"I saw her right before I got in the shower. She seemed fine. I'll probably work her in the morning while the class is practicing with their dogs." She stepped back. "Did you want to come in? It would only take me a moment to throw some clothes on."

He willed his feet to stay put. "No, don't bother. I was just about to turn in myself." The scent of wildflowers rose from her skin like a sensual cloud, surrounding him. He swallowed thickly.

"I just brewed some tea," she said. "There's enough for two if you'd like a cup."

Nick despised tea. It was a woman's drink. Something his mother used to take for cramps. "Sounds good," he found himself saying as he brushed past her into the small apartment. "But you don't have to change." His tattered self-control hoped she would; the part of him that appreciated her appealing disarray wanted her to remain in the inexplicably sexy pink robe.

For a moment, she hesitated and he thought she was going to say something. Then she obviously reconsidered. Their gazes held and a moment of sharp awareness passed between them, leaving Nick shaken.

"Sit down," she said, fleeing. "I'll be right back."

Erin closed the bedroom door behind her and leaned against it. What was wrong with her? Hands shaking, she threw on underwear, sweats and an oversized tee-shirt. Then she took a deep breath and returned to the tiny living room.

Nick stood with his broad back to her, looking out the window. He turned when he heard her muffled footsteps.

His gaze drifted the length of her before seeking her face. A half smile played at the corners of his mouth.

"Nice outfit." His tone was dry.

Erin felt herself blushing. "I grabbed the first thing I found," she said defensively.

He shook his head. "No, I mean it. On you, anything looks

good." He took a step forward, then stopped. Erin realized she had
moved toward him, too. She glanced at the kitchen counter, where
the teapot sat like a chubby chaperone.

"The tea," she exclaimed with a bright smile. "I'll get it."

Nick took another step toward her, reluctantly, as if he were
being pulled against his will.

"Forget the tea," he said, lifting his hands. One touched her hair.
Erin angled her head toward him without thinking. His other hand
came up, skated over her chin, tipped it up while he searched her
eyes. Her feet moved of their own accord, carrying her closer, until
their thighs brushed. Heat spread through her.

His hands cradled her head gently. She thought she felt a tremor
shake them, couldn't be sure. She was trembling herself as his gaze
went unerringly to her mouth. His pupils expanded, darkening his
green eyes. He leaned closer. She bent her head back. Waited,
breathless.

"You don't know how badly I want this," he muttered. "And
how hard I tried to resist."

Erin's mind was too confused to sort out what he had just told
her. Instead, she reached up to grip his arms, feeling the hard muscles, and held on tight.

The first touch of his lips was gentle, a sweet brushing of warm,
sensitive flesh. It banished any niggling second thoughts from
plucking at her attention. She pressed her mouth to his, swallowing
a sound of pleasure.

Before she'd begun to get enough of him, he lifted his head.
Without her consent, her hands slid across his shoulders and pulled
his head back down.

Nick groaned, a haunting, primitive sound that kicked up Erin's
heart rate. Then his open mouth covered hers, hot and wet, in a
kiss so unlike the first that it shocked her to her toes. Helpless,
she responded, parting her lips for the invasion of his tongue. Desire
roared through her like a runaway train. Her fingers burrowed in
his hair. Her heart slammed against her chest. Vaguely, she felt his
arms tighten around her. Then, as she became lost in sensation,
wave after wave of pleasure washing over her, he pulled away so
abruptly that she almost fell.

Erin's eyes popped open. Nick was staring at her, an expression
of accusation on his face. What had she done? What was he think-

ing? Did he somehow hold her responsible for what had just happened between them?

Before she could utter a word, he made a harsh sound as he thrust her away from him, whirled and headed for the door.

"Where are you going?" she asked foolishly.

"This is a mistake." His voice was husky. "I shouldn't have come here tonight. I'm sorry."

Confused and annoyed by his hasty retreat, Erin snapped, "You're undoubtedly right."

Nick froze, one hand on the doorknob. He glanced at her over his shoulder, expression tortured. "Trust me, lady, I'm the last man you need to get mixed up with."

Erin stared after him as he yanked open the door and bolted through it, slamming it shut behind him. She might have agreed with him, might have decided once and for all that he was too much a jerk to bother with. Except for one thing.

Except for the shadow of pain she had glimpsed in his haunted green eyes. Maybe her real mistake had been in letting him leave.

No, she decided with a shake of her head. The last thing she needed was to get emotionally involved with someone like Nick. Someone else with problems. She had enough of her own.

The students were doing well, beginning to function as teams with their canine friends. The dogs slept in the apartment units with their humans now, a step that always seemed to hasten the bonding process so necessary for a successful pairing.

"How did it go last night?" Erin asked the group when they had assembled after breakfast. She glanced around. "Jane?"

The older woman beamed as she stroked her dog's head. "Ranger helped me get ready for bed last night. He retrieved the toothpaste tube when I dropped it, turned the light out. I'm sure I won't need the attendant tonight." Her voice carried a note of pride in her own independence that had been missing before.

"Terrific," Erin said with an encouraging nod. "Freddie?"

The little boy looked around at the others. "We did good," he said. "Queenie put my dirty clothes in the hamper."

The others chuckled.

"Lucy?" Erin asked, trying not to think about Nick leaning against the back wall. He hadn't taken his eyes off her.

Lucy hesitated, glancing at her brother. "Max did everything a paid attendant could have done," she said in a tone that bordered on belligerence. "He and I make a great team."

Erin watched Nick's brows rise, but his expression, which revealed nothing of his thoughts, remained the same. She wondered what he might be thinking about his sister and her determination to regain her independence.

"Well," Erin said, returning her attention to the class. "So far, so good. If there aren't any other questions or comments, we'll move on to today's lesson."

As Nick watched her from his place at the back of the room, she ran a hand through her hair and began explaining the commands they would learn and practice with the dogs today. She was wearing her familiar uniform of jeans and a tee-shirt. This one was lavender with the words "Skagit Valley Tulip Festival" in faded letters across the swells of her breasts.

Nick remembered the way she had felt in his arms the night before, and shifted uncomfortably. What had he been thinking? Or had he? Now that he knew how good she tasted and felt, it was going to be harder than ever to stay away from her. Especially at the center.

She was everywhere he turned. Counseling students, working with the dogs, talking to the attendants or greeting the occasional visitor who came to inspect the facility and perhaps make a donation. Erin's dedication fascinated him; her energy and enthusiasm attracted him. The memory of the kisses they had shared made him burn. He admired her singular devotion to her cause, and he wondered what kept her going. What powered all that energy that seemed to radiate from her like sunshine?

And why did he care? Lucy was the one he should be concerned about. Lucy who thought a trained dog was the answer to her prayers to make everything the way it used to be. Before the accident. Before an instant's inattention on Nick's part had sentenced his baby sister to life in a wheelchair.

A sudden restlessness took hold of him. Barely aware of Erin's startled expression, he strode to the door and jerked it open, looking only for escape.

What he found was Darren, cleaning out a dahlia bed that had been killed by the night frost.

"Hey," the other man greeted him as Nick hesitated. "Just the guy I was looking for. Got time to give me a hand today?"

Nick shrugged. Perhaps a few chores would take his mind off Erin and the soft feel of her lips on his.

"Sure. What do you need?"

Darren hefted the clippers, his weathered face creasing into a grin. "Funny you should ask," he replied in a teasing tone.

"Basketball?" Erin echoed, glancing up from the sandwich on her lunch plate. "You played basketball in high school, Nick?"

His expression became guarded. "Yeah, I did. I played varsity for three years, why?"

She raised one brow. "I was a forward on the girls' team at Roosevelt."

His chin came up in an unmistakable gesture of male arrogance. "Girls' basketball," he said in a scornful tone. "Big difference."

Erin pushed her plate away, enjoying the exchange. Aware that the others were watching the two of them closely. She hadn't seen Nick alone since he had kissed her. Was he avoiding her deliberately?

"Not so different," she contradicted. "We played hard and I wasn't a bad shot."

He made a disparaging sound in his throat. Freddie giggled.

"I think he needs to be taken down a peg," Anna muttered in a low voice. She knew that Erin often took out her frustrations on the hoop behind the dining room.

"Think you're hot?" Nick asked.

Erin shrugged. "I get by." For a moment, she could almost forget the sensual attraction that sizzled between them. "Besides, I have youth on my side," she added coolly. "Your high school years must be a distant memory at this point in time."

Nick's grin faltered; his eyes narrowed. "You wound me. Are you implying that I'm too old to keep up with you?" he asked. "A mere woman?"

Jane hooted and Freddie banged his fist on the table. Darren smothered a chuckle as Anna elbowed him.

"Watch yourself, Nick," Lucy called out.

Nick's expression was pure challenge. "I could dribble rings around you, McKenzie."

Erin pushed back her chair and rose to her feet. "Prove it, Blackwood," she said, as the others egged her on.

"How?"

"There's a hoop out back. How about a little game of one on one?" She wasn't worried. She'd always been fast on her feet and seemed to have a sixth sense when it came to hitting the basket. Now some inner compulsion drove her on. She didn't question it. Beating Nick at something physical was too tempting to resist.

"Now?" He looked surprised.

"Why not?"

He glanced around at the attentive faces. Obviously, it went against his macho grain to turn down a challenge.

"I don't have the right shoes," he said.

"Oh, give me a break," Jane groaned.

Erin turned to Darren. "What size do you wear?"

"Eleven." He glanced at Nick. "I've got high tops."

"Good enough." Nick didn't take his eyes off Erin. She barely resisted the urge to squirm. "Could I borrow them?"

Darren slid his chair out. "Sure thing. I'll be right back."

Erin watched him leave the room as the first tiny niggles of misgiving began squirming around in her stomach like giant tadpoles. What had she gotten herself into? What if Nick whipped her? Made her look foolish? She would never hear the end of it. Then her chin came up.

No, he might give her a run for her money, but she'd beat him or die trying. Perhaps it would be more prudent not to trounce his male ego too badly, but Erin was past thinking about doing the prudent thing. She was savoring the idea of creaming him, making him admit on one level at least that she was someone to reckon with. Someone who affected him as strongly as he affected her.

Before Erin could say anything, Darren was back with a pair of athletic shoes in one hand and a basketball in the other.

"Come, children," he said. "Time for recess."

Erin looked at him but he merely grinned. Did he think she was nuts? "Let's get this over with so we can start the afternoon lesson," she said, hiding her sudden nervousness.

"You shouldn't be so eager to bring about your ignominious defeat," Nick said, pulling off his shoes and slipping into the ones Darren gave him. He stood up and took a few experimental steps, bobbing and weaving around an imaginary opponent.

"These will do."

Erin was already wearing tennis shoes. Adrenaline was starting to flow. She took the basketball from Darren.

"See you outside," she said, speculating that Nick's traditional, slightly chauvinistic attitude wouldn't lend itself well to defeat. Wondering what she was trying to prove.

Jane, Lucy, Freddie and the others followed her outside with the dogs and formed a ragged ring around the hoop. The women, even Lucy, backed Erin while Freddie cheered Nick on and Darren remained neutral.

"This shouldn't take long," Nick said as he took the ball and dribbled it experimentally while Erin did a few warmup stretches. "You won't get a hand on the ball."

Erin straightened. "Be prepared to eat your words."

Nick's gaze never wavered as he bounced the ball. "Care to make it worth my while?"

She frowned. "What have you got in mind?"

He thought a moment while she held her breath. "Dinner in Seattle," he said. "Winner's choice, loser pays."

She didn't know if spending another evening with him was wise. Was surprised he'd even suggested it.

"Chicken?" he taunted.

She grabbed the ball, surprising him. "Deal. First one to score ten baskets wins."

"Deal," he said. "And I have to warn you, I have a real fondness for expensive food. Especially when someone else is picking up the tab."

"I hope you brought your gold card," Erin replied as she approached the free throw line. "You're going to need it."

Their gazes met, clashed. Nick's smile was brimming with confidence. "First one to miss a free throw, the other starts. Watch your step, honey. You're way out of your league."

Uneasily, Erin wondered if he was more right than he could possibly know.

Six

The score was tied, eight baskets each, and Nick had the ball. His dark blue tee-shirt was damp across his chest, and sweat ran down his face.

"It's all over but the shouting, McKenzie," he taunted. "Dust off your bank card."

"In your dreams." Erin was winded. He was good; quick and strong. She had managed to stay with him through sheer grit and nerve, taking advantage of his reluctance to jostle her by crowding close and dogging his steps. She could feel the perspiration trickling between her breasts like little crawly critters on her skin.

"Watch and learn." He faked a move to the right, then slipped by her as she scrambled to change direction. Vaguely, she was aware of Freddie cheering him on. She recovered and shadowed Nick. He charged the basket, leaping high, but she stayed with him. Deflecting the ball when he shot, she grabbed it out of the air.

"Nice move," he gasped as they came down.

Whirling, she sprang toward the hoop as he did the same, blocking her body with his. In midair, she did her best to twist away from him, but they collided, hard, as the ball slipped from her grasp.

Shaken, Nick landed with his feet spread wide. He grabbed for Erin but missed.

Knocked off balance, she hit the ground on one foot. The leg that took her weight crumpled beneath her, the ankle turning awkwardly and then giving way altogether. Her shoulder smacked against the blacktop and she cried out.

He saw the pain flash across her face as she curled her body into a ball.

"Erin!" Nick dropped to one knee beside her. "Are you okay?" The others crowded close, echoing his concern.

"Give her room!" He was gasping for breath. Erin had been a tougher opponent than he had expected. It took everything in him to keep up.

Erin turned over, groaning. Her face was pale. Nick stuck out a hand.

"Can you sit up?"

She nodded and pulled herself up.

"Get your breath," he said. "You took a hard fall."

"I'm okay." Her voice shook.

She started to rise and he helped her, taking her weight. He could see that her ankle was already swelling.

"Perhaps you'd better—"

She moaned as she stepped on that foot and immediately sank back down to the ground.

"It's my ankle," she groaned as tears of pain filled her eyes.

Nick touched the swollen joint carefully and she flinched away. "Ow."

"I'll get some ice," Darren offered and hurried off.

"Sorry. I'll bet you've sprained it." Nick felt bad. He never should have agreed to play. He'd been too rough, knocking her down like he had. He should have pulled back and let her win.

"It's not your fault." Erin closed her eyes for a moment as nausea surged through her stomach. She *would not* disgrace herself further by being sick!

Nick untied her shoe and slipped it off as she bit her lip to keep another groan from escaping.

Darren handed him a plastic bag full of ice. "It's swelling pretty fast."

"I'd better go to the clinic," Erin told him as Nick set the bag carefully on her ankle. "Would you drive me?"

"I'll take you," Nick said. "It was my fault that it happened."

"Nonsense." Erin's tone was sharp with annoyance. The last thing she wanted was for Nick to feel guilty about *her*. She swallowed. "I probably only twisted it."

"Better have it x-rayed and taped, anyway," Nick insisted.

"I have a class to teach," Erin argued, unsure just why she was being so stubborn. "I can go later."

"No way," Darren said, exchanging glances with Nick over her head.

Erin felt like a child among adults. Before she could speak again, Nick asked, "Darren, can you teach the class? Then I can take Grace, here, to the clinic."

"Grace!" she exclaimed, insulted. He was the one who had plowed into her.

"Good idea. I can handle things here." Darren rose, ignoring Erin's squawk of protest, and turned away as if everything had been settled to his satisfaction. "Come on, guys," he said to the tiny group of spectators. "Let's get started."

"Just a minute," Erin protested again, but no one listened. They were following Darren as if he were the Pied Piper. "How do you like that for loyalty," she muttered to no one in particular as Nick bent over her.

"What do you think you're doing!" she cried when he scooped her effortlessly into his arms as if she weighed no more than dandelion fluff.

"Taking you to the doctor," he said, straightening. "Hang onto the ice bag. I'll put you in the van and get the keys."

"Not necessary," Darren called, pausing to open the passenger door so that Nick could dump her onto the seat. She scrambled to rearrange herself as Darren tossed the keys to Nick.

"You don't have to do this," she grumbled when Nick came around to the driver's side and got in. "I can manage without you."

"Sure, you can." Nick started the engine. "I'm the one who ran into you, remember? Now, give me directions to the clinic."

She told him where it was and sank back in the padded seat, swallowing another moan. "You hardly touched me," she argued after a few moments of silence. "I was much too quick for you."

He glanced at her, brows raised in disbelief, but remained silent. She tried to shift her foot and pain ran up her leg like an electric shock. "Damn," she grumbled. "I was winning, too."

"Hah," he said, slowing to turn a corner. "Did you land on your head? The score was tied, McKenzie."

"No," she snapped. "I didn't land on my head. I hit my shoulder." She rotated it experimentally. It was stiff but not too sore. "I'll probably have a bruise."

"I'm sorry," he said, pulling into the parking lot of the clinic. "I didn't mean to knock you down, honest." He flashed her a repentant grin before he slammed his door and circled the front of the van.

Erin had her door open and was in the process of getting out when he reached her.

"Stay put," he commanded, "while I get a wheelchair."

"I don't need a wheelchair," she said petulantly. Erin was hardly ever sick, and she hated being dependent on anyone else. That was probably why she believed so strongly in the service dogs; she was aware of just how important any measure of independence was.

Nick glared at her, obviously exasperated. "It's either a wheelchair or I'll carry you in," he threatened. "And I won't be as gentle as the last time."

She pictured herself hanging over his shoulder in a fireman's carry. "Oh, all right. I'll wait for a wheelchair."

"Promise?" he asked. His eyes gleamed.

She stared but he merely waited. Her ankle throbbed, reminding her that she needed medical attention.

"I promise." She glared at him, but he chuckled softly as he turned away. While he was gone, Erin removed the bag of ice and looked at her swollen ankle.

Great. This was just what she needed when she was in the middle of boot camp. How was she supposed to manage her responsibilities now?

"I don't have the time for crutches," she grumbled as they drove home from the clinic. "My schedule is too busy."

"I'll help," Nick said without looking at her.

"Thanks." Erin was feeling much more subdued. She'd given her ankle only a medium sprain, the doctor had told her after she waited what seemed like forever for the x-rays to be developed. She had to use crutches for a few days and stay off her feet as much as possible.

Nick slowed the van, pulling into the center's parking lot. "I mean it," he said, as he killed the engine and looked at her. "I'll help with whatever you need. It's the least I can do."

All of a sudden, Erin felt ashamed of the way she had been acting. Her injury wasn't Nick's fault any more than her own. It had just been one of those dumb accidents.

"I meant what I said, too," she told him sincerely. "Thank you for taking me to the clinic and for waiting all that time. I do appreciate it."

Nick waved her thanks away with a casual gesture. "I'm just sorry we didn't have a chance to finish the game," he drawled, getting out of the van. "I was looking forward to dinner at the Space Needle." He shut the door before Erin could think of a suitable reply.

"What makes you think you would have won?" she sputtered when he came around to her side and removed her crutches. "We were tied when I fell."

He shrugged as he adjusted them. Then he held them out to her, his grin maddening. "Yeah, but you were tiring. I could tell." He grasped her wrists and helped her carefully out of the van. Erin barely noticed, so busy was she sputtering at his brash overconfidence.

"How can you say I was tiring?" she demanded.

"Your tongue was hanging out."

She ignored his outrageous comment. "I was not tiring! I had plenty of energy left and I would have run rings around you. When my ankle's better we'll have a rematch and—"

"Oh, no!" he exclaimed, backing away to give her room to maneuver on the crutches. "I don't think that's a good idea at all."

"Now who's the chicken?" she taunted, taking a couple of experimental steps. No way was she going to allow him to keep insisting that he would have won.

"You're back!" Lucy exclaimed, leading a wheelchair welcoming committee toward them. "How's your ankle?"

Erin glanced at Nick, promising with her eyes that the discussion wasn't over yet.

"It's okay," she told Lucy. "Just a little sprain. I have to use crutches for a couple of days."

"The doctor said a few days," Nick corrected her, "not a couple."

Erin ignored him. "How did class go?" she asked Darren, who came up behind the students.

"Fine."

"Good." Erin moved forward awkwardly but with determination. "I'll take over now."

"You'll do no such thing," Nick corrected her again. "The doctor told you to take a pain pill and have a rest when you got back here."

Erin glared at him. "I don't have time. Who's the boss around here, anyway?"

Nick's grin was downright roguish. He leaned forward and touched her nose with his finger. Erin forced herself not to flinch away.

"Honey," he told her, "I'd say that, until the doctor gives you the green light, you and I are a team."

On the evening after Erin's injury, Nick sat in the one uncomfortable chair in his apartment and stared at the wall. He had just gotten off the phone from his daily call to his father, who was running the company during Nick's absence. Despite the usual disasters and lesser problems, the business seemed to be humming along as smoothly as any construction outfit could in the face of the constant challenges of unpredictable weather, lost shipments of supplies, equipment breakdowns, labor problems and delays caused by county inspectors and government red tape.

The cement sent to one job that day had been too wet, the custom-made skylights for a second were nowhere to be found, and the bricklayers on yet another had walked off the job. One of the ditch witches they were leasing had broken down and a replacement wasn't available until the next morning. A plumbing inspector wasn't happy with the soldering on a section of pipe a subcontractor had installed and wouldn't allow the sheetrock to be put in until it was redone.

Nick ran a hand through his hair and did his best to ignore the restless itch he felt at not being able to handle things himself. His father had asked if he could make it home for a couple of days. Nick had put him off.

He knew that his old man could cope without him. Had done more than just cope in building the company from scratch in the years before Nick had taken over. Burt Blackwood was a man who believed in hard work, in shouldering responsibility without complaint and in accepting blame when it was due. In dealing with life's lumps without whining.

He and Nick had never discussed Nick's feelings about Lucy's accident. Nick knew that, as far as Burt Blackwood was concerned, a man did what he had to do.

Nick's thoughts shifted abruptly to Erin and the events of that afternoon. To the injury he had dealt her on the basketball court. He seemed to have a talent for hurting the women he . . .

Nick's thoughts faltered. Just how did he feel about Erin? His mind shied away from the answer. He told himself the only reason he had insisted on carrying Erin to the van and driving her to the doctor was because he had been responsible for her sprained ankle. Not because he had been glad of the excuse to hold her in his arms. Not because he would take advantage of any opportunity to be alone with her.

Not because he was attracted to her.

Hell, he admitted that much, at least to himself. But he could handle it.

Once they were back from the clinic, he had done his best to help Erin as he had promised he would. He insisted she rest, but she had ignored him. Instead, she had taken over the class for the rest of the day.

He tried to wait on her at dinner. She let him carry her tray, but that was all. He had offered to assist her at whatever she planned to do in the evening, but she had laughed and dismissed him as if he were no more help than a pesky child. On top of everything else, as soon as Erin limped out of sight on her crutches, Lucy had approached and demanded to know what was going on between Nick and the boss.

"Nothing," he had assured his nosy younger sister.

"Hah!" she replied. "I know sparks when I see them."

He'd tried innocence and, when that hadn't worked, annoyance. She refused to be dissuaded.

"Come on," she coaxed. "Admit it. You've got a thing for her."

Only when he tried to reassure Lucy that he would never abandon her had he achieved the desired affect of distracting her from the subject of Erin.

"I don't want or need your single-minded devotion," Lucy insisted. "You have the right to a life of your own. Why won't you accept that I don't want you at my beck and call?"

Before he could reply, she had turned her chair away. But not before he saw the tears in her eyes, their shape and color so similar to his own. When, oh when, would his head-strong little sister realize that he only had her best interests at heart?

Now, for a long moment, Nick contemplated the toe of Darren's athletic shoe, which he hadn't thought to return, along with the fantasy of being free from responsibilities, free to explore the idea of some kind of relationship with Erin for the weeks that remained of his stay in Monroe—without considering the consequences to anyone but her and himself. It wasn't the fear that he would hate to leave her when the time was up, he told himself, it was just the knowledge that he had accepted the responsibilities he did have. Wishing things could be different was only an unproductive waste of time. Not to mention an activity his father would have looked on as a far less than manly thing to do.

Nick rose and glanced around the bare unit that would be his home until Lucy was ready to return to Eugene. Maybe a fast walk around the grounds before he turned in might relax him. At least the chill wind that had sprung up might blow the unwanted thoughts from his head so he could get some sleep that night.

As each day that Erin spent on crutches passed, she felt more dependent on Nick. Despite his apparently unending store of patience and cheer, the realization that she needed him, at least temporarily, didn't sweeten her mood.

"I appreciate your help since I sprained my ankle," she admitted grudgingly as he drove her to a fund raising luncheon in Edmonds. She was scheduled to give a talk and slide show to a coalition of local businessmen in hopes they would include a regular donation to the center in their annual budget.

"No problem," Nick replied, steering carefully down the steep, winding road into town. "Just be sure to cue me when you want the slides changed."

"I can do that myself," Erin protested, not for the first time. Nick had been tireless when it came to helping with a school visit up in Bellingham the day before. He had managed the dogs, the students and the props like a pro. Despite Erin's lack of mobility, the visit had gone quite well.

At today's luncheon, she wouldn't have to worry about the dogs. She always took at least one of them on a school visit, and yesterday had been no exception. Business lunches, on the other hand, seemed to call for slides and handouts rather than the actual presence of the animals themselves. Just as they called for a suit rather than her usual uniform of jeans, tee-shirt and orange windbreaker.

"No point in your doing the slides yourself when you have me to help you," Nick stated with irritating male logic as he signalled for a turn. "I don't mind." His gaze strayed to Erin's nylon-clad legs below the straight skirt of her turquoise suit. With the outfit, she wore medium-heeled pumps, despite Nick's warning that she might reinjure her ankle, silver hoop earrings and a generous misting of the cologne that Anna and Darren had given her for Christmas.

But *I* mind, she thought in reaction to Nick's words. She wondered whether he approved of her spiffed-up appearance. He had said nothing, but she thought she noticed his eyes widen in approval. Or surprise that she was capable of dressing like a real woman.

She found Nick's appearance, in baggy slacks and a striped shirt with the sleeves rolled back, a significant distraction. His company had given her a painful glimpse of what her work would be like with a real partner to help. Not a business partner like Anna, but a romantic partner. As in boyfriend, lover, husband. Someone who shared her vision as well as her life.

Now where had that thought come from?

She had no more time to ponder the idea; they had arrived at the restaurant where her presentation was to take place.

"Can you manage?" Nick asked solicitously. At her impatient nod, he said, "Why don't you go on in and I'll bring the equipment." He indicated her briefcase, which had been a present from her parents, and the box of slides.

"Thanks." She grabbed the hated crutches.

As soon as the excellent seafood lunch and Erin's talk were both over, Nick began gathering up the flyers and brochures that she had put out earlier. As he did so, he kept a suspicious eye on the chairman of the businessmens' coalition, a tall, tanned man with sandy brown hair and a bushy mustache Nick would have loved to rip out with his bare hands.

What business did this bum, who Nick thought he heard someone say was a lawyer, have standing so close to Erin? Did he have to gaze at her with such rapt attention, hanging onto her every word like a lovesick fool?

Silently, Nick gave the other man, who reminded him of a well-dressed male mannequin in his six-hundred dollar suit, about ten more seconds to back off before Nick gave in to the burning urge to intervene. Was Erin getting enough air or was Mister Congeniality using it all up?

While Nick fumed silently, his itchy fingers managed to knock a pile of colorful brochures onto the floor. Swearing under his breath, he bent to pick them up. As he did so, he noticed that Erin was laughing at something the lawyer must have said. She was probably only playing to his ego, Nick told himself; in the hopes that a little friendliness on her part might oil the skids for a donation from the group the man headed.

Nick straightened, took a deep, cleansing breath and slammed Erin's briefcase shut. Hands curled into fists, temper simmering, he advanced on the pair, baring his teeth in what he assumed would pass as a smile.

"That's a lovely offer," he heard Erin tell the man who was watching her with the beady-eyed gaze of one of Edmond's many hungry sea gulls. Nick's fingers twitched as he subdued, but just barely, the urge to grab that expensive suit by the nap of its well-tailored neck and give it a healthy yank.

"But I'm afraid I'll have to ask you for a rain check. My current class takes all my time." Erin's voice sounded way too friendly.

Nick relaxed his fingers and took another deep, steadying breath.

"Surely you have weekends off," the other man persisted in a wheedling tone as Nick came to them and stopped.

Erin glanced up, her eyes widening slightly, then returned her attention to the other man. She must have seen something disturbing in Nick's expression, he realized. Her voice faltered as she made a non-committal response, and she cleared her throat.

Nick hastily wiped all emotion from his face and replaced it with a bland smile.

"Ready, boss?" he urged her as she shifted her grip on her crutches. "We're running late."

Erin glanced at him again. "We are?" She looked puzzled. No wonder. Nick knew of no other engagements that afternoon.

"Oh, yes," she said, frown clearing. "You're right." She beamed in his general direction, but her gaze failed to connect with his.

"I'm so glad your group invited me," she told her admirer. "It's been a treat meeting all of you, and I hope you'll decide to include the center in your annual budget."

The man's smile reminded Nick of a counterfeit coin, worthless as well as phony.

"We loved having you," he said, as Nick chafed at the possible double meaning of his words. "And you can be sure we'll go over the information you left with us very carefully." He placed his free hand over Erin's on the rung of her crutch.

Nick barely suppressed a grin when she managed to shift away from his touch without missing a beat.

"Have your secretary call me if you need any more information about the center."

Nick shifted impatiently from one foot to the other.

"And I'm really sorry about dinner," Erin added, studiously ignoring his fidgeting.

The lawyer drew out a slim gold pen and a business card. Writing quickly on the back of it, he handed the card to Erin.

"Here's my private number, if your situation changes," he told her.

Nick cleared his throat. Erin tucked the card into her pocket with a murmur of thanks and glanced at her watch. "Oh, dear." After a round of good-byes and handshakes, she and Nick broke away from the group.

"What are we late for?" she demanded as soon as he shut the door to the banquet room behind them.

"I thought you wanted to get out of there," Nick replied innocently. "I was just trying to help."

When she turned to stare at him, he expected to see annoyance, even disapproval, on her face. Instead, her eyes twinkled with amusement.

"I see," was all she said, as she turned and began to make her way laboriously toward the car.

Nick would have liked to ask what she found so amusing, but

his gut instinct told him he might not appreciate the answer. Instead, he hurried on ahead of her and opened the passenger door.

On the drive home, Erin found her amusement at Nick's possible jealousy evaporating in view of his continued bad mood.

"Do you disapprove of my methods for soliciting donations for the center?" she finally asked, to break the silence that had become awkward.

Nick glanced her way, but didn't answer for so long that she thought he wasn't going to bother.

"I guess I would have disapproved more if you had accepted the guy's offer," he admitted finally, staring at the road.

Erin debated whether to be offended at his implication. Instead, she chose to find his admission flattering, and proceeded to spend the rest of the trip back to the center describing the addition she wanted to build as soon as she found the money.

When the two of them were getting out of the van, Anna, minus the wheelchair she often used, met them waving an invitation. She was leaning on a wooden cane.

"We're all invited to a reception for the physically chal-lenged that's being sponsored by one of the Everett service clubs," she said. "It will be a terrific experience for the class and their dogs."

"When is it?" Erin asked. The luncheon had tired her more than she wanted to admit. Thank goodness she had a doctor's appointment in two days and fully expected to get rid of the hated crutches then.

"It's this Sunday afternoon." Anna walked to the office with Erin and Nick.

Erin couldn't suppress a groan. She had planned to spend Sunday with her parents at their home on Camano Island.

"You don't have to go, do you?" Nick asked. "That's your only day off."

"We'll see." Undoubtedly, her enthusiasm would return with her second wind.

"Darren and I can play chaperone, if you have other plans," Anna offered.

Erin smiled gratefully at her friend. "I'll let you know. Thanks for offering."

* * *

At dinner that evening, the reception was discussed thoroughly. "Will there be lots of food?" Freddie wanted to know.

"I might meet some other women my age there," Jane mused.

While Erin watched, Nick glanced at Lucy, who was sitting on the other side of Freddie and Kim, the housekeeper. "It should be fun," he offered.

"Are you planning to go?" Lucy demanded. "Erin will be off crutches by then. She won't need your help, and neither will I."

Her rudeness surprised Erin. She felt bad for Nick, whose cheeks had darkened at Lucy's comment.

"Hey," he said in a tone that sounded falsely hearty. "What else do I have to do on Sunday than take my favorite girl to a party?"

Conversation around the table ground to a halt. Nick had to be hurt by Lucy's attitude. Erin ached for him and the obvious embarrassment he refused to acknowledge. Right or wrong, his intentions were only the best.

Lucy leaned forward, about to reply to him when Erin, acting totally on impulse, cut in.

"Actually," she blurted as the others swiveled to stare at her, "I was planning to invite Nick up to my folks' house on Sunday."

Seven

"Mom always goes overboard on lunch," Erin told Nick as she climbed over a driftwood log on the beach below her parents' house and waited for him to follow.

"She's a great cook," he replied, crossing the log and taking her hand. "Can you cook?" His eyes gleamed with interest.

Erin laughed. "Not as well as Mom." She glanced around the deserted beach, hugging herself. "I wish it was warmer today."

The wind had a raw edge to it, and whitecaps dotted the waters of Utsaladdy Bay. Clouds in a hundred shades of gray filled the sky. Erin was wearing a stocking cap and gloves as well as her thick parka.

"I like to walk on the beach after a winter storm," Nick said, staring out across the water. "It has a certain primitive appeal." He turned to look at Erin through narrowed eyes. His windblown hair looked as if it had been combed with restless fingers and his cheeks were buffed with color.

Erin began walking and Nick fell in beside her. The tide was partway out, exposing an expanse of wet sand that made walking easier than did the loose rocks further up the beach.

"Just think," she mused, "this view is unchanged from the one our ancestors saw when they stood on this spot."

"Except for all those houses over on Whidbey," Nick drawled, pointing.

Erin swatted at his arm. "I meant the water and the sky," she said, spreading her arms wide. "And the wind and the elements. They're unchanged."

"Except for the pollution." Nick ducked away playfully, avoiding another swat.

"Have you no romance in your soul?" Erin demanded. "No imagination?" She shook her head. "Pollution," she muttered, beginning to walk again.

Her parents liked Nick, she could tell. Her father was boisterous and outgoing, her mother more quiet, slower to decide. Erin knew, though, that they were probably full of questions, discussing him while they did the dishes together. Erin had offered to help, but her mother shooed her and Nick outside, insisting they walk off lunch instead.

"You don't have enough time away from the center as it is," she had grumbled. "Take a walk. Forget your responsibilities for an hour."

That was just what Erin was trying to do, although having Nick beside her made it more difficult to banish the center from her thoughts completely.

"No romance!" he echoed, grabbing her arm. "Lady, I'll show you romance."

Erin barely had time to notice that the beach was deserted except for themselves as he swept her into a bearlike embrace and bent her back over his arm. She clutched at his shoulders. Nick, too, was wearing a heavy jacket, along with leather gloves borrowed from Erin's father. His mouth, when it came down on hers, was cold. His nose, too.

His mouth heated quickly on hers. As he straightened, pulling her up with him, Erin's good sense dissolved as if it had never existed. She kissed him back, savoring the warmth and softness of his lips. Then she linked her gloved fingers around his neck and pressed herself against him.

Nick lifted his head and Erin moaned a protest, but he only changed angle and kissed her again. He pulled her body closer still, grasping her hips and slipping his denim-covered leg between hers. Sensation rippled through her as she felt the hard muscle of his thigh pressed intimately against her.

His mouth became more avid, his tongue delving deep, caressing, tangling with hers. Erin's arms tightened. Her tongue followed his as he groaned deep in his throat. He pulled away to bury his mouth in the warm hollow of her neck above the bulky collar of her parka. His face was hot against her chilled skin, his breath dancing along her nerve endings like busy fingers.

His hands locked on her hips, holding her tight against his male heat. Erin's legs trembled with reaction as she dragged her eyes open and stared up at him, dazed.

Nick glanced around, expression rueful. "There's never a cave around when you need one," he said with a half smile. "We'd better start walking before I stop caring where we are."

His arm anchored Erin close to his side. She felt a chill where her body had been pressed against his. For a moment, the wind seemed bitterly cold and much stronger than before. Then she took a deep breath and glanced away.

"Good idea." Her voice was a high squeak, and she cleared her throat.

Nick leaned his already cold cheek to hers, making her jump. "Having trouble talking?" he asked in a tone laced with amusement.

Erin didn't know whether to be relieved or annoyed by his teasing attitude. What they shared had been monumental to her, had altered her feelings about men and desire and had changed her in some fundamental way she didn't yet understand. Apparently, the exchange meant nothing more to Nick than a handshake. That hurt. She hoped he had no idea how strongly it affected her.

Deciding she should be grateful for his attempt at lightness, Erin managed a smile. "Maybe kissing always leaves me speechless."

For a moment, his eyes darkened and his smile faded. "Are you trying to tell me you always respond like that?" His fingers grasped her chin, hard. "Are you?"

Her gaze faltered. She wasn't very good at lying.

"You can't expect me to answer that!" she exclaimed instead. "A girl has to have a few secrets."

His smile returned, slightly skewed. "I guess that's answer enough," he said after a moment, voice brimming with male satisfaction. "I knew I wasn't in this alone."

She remained silent, refusing to either agree or disagree. He would be gone soon, she had to remember that. Kissing him would be just a pleasant memory. Neither of them had anything more than pleasant memories to leave with each other.

Unable to think of some harmless subject with which to break the silence, Erin began walking again.

"How's your ankle?" Nick asked, jamming his hands into the deep pockets of his jacket as he moved beside her. "Maybe we shouldn't go too far."

Erin glanced down at the ankle she had recently injured. "It's fine." In truth, she had all but forgotten about it. Earlier, Nick had cautioned her to be careful on their way down the short, steep path to the beach, but it didn't hurt. She wondered what the doctor would say about her walking among the driftwood and slippery rocks, then dismissed the thought. She would have risked both ankles for that kiss.

They walked in silence for a little while. She could feel Nick's retreat, back behind the wall he usually kept wrapped around him. Far ahead of them on the stretch of wet, glistening sand that was dotted with gulls, were two figures, too small to see if they were approaching or retreating. Part of Erin was glad for their presence, part wished for total privacy and a few more moments spent in Nick's arms.

"Lucy's doing better in class," she said, as they turned to go back the way they had come. "She and Max are getting along well."

"She wanted to be a model before she was hurt," Nick volunteered, looking up at the sky that went from the palest pearl gray above the water to a dark, glowering purple along the jagged silhouette of mountains to the east.

"She would have made a good model," Erin said. "She certainly has the looks for it."

"I wonder if she would have stayed with modeling," Nick muttered, almost as if he were speaking to himself. "When she found out what hard work it's supposed to be." He glanced down at Erin and she could see the shadows of guilt and sadness in his face. "I guess we'll never know."

"There are a lot of things Lucy will be able to do with her life," Erin argued. She wanted to add that Max would help, but didn't. She knew that Nick still didn't accept the idea of a dog making a difference.

"But not modeling," he said, the bitterness back in his voice.

"Maybe not," she agreed. "But other things."

He didn't answer. They were back to the spot where the path went up the hill. He reached out a hand to help Erin over the logs. She grasped his gloved fingers. His touch felt impersonal, as if he had already left her.

The next day the class discussed Sunday's reception and went to a fast food outlet for lunch. Erin's regular volunteers were back, so Nick didn't accompany them. Freddie knocked over his soda, but that was the only mishap. When they got back to the center, Erin showed them the new commands they were to learn.

" 'Speak' and 'quiet' are easy," she said, demonstrating with Ranger. He barked on command and stopped when she indicated. "That's it, Ranger," Erin said, using the phrase that told him he had done the right thing. She patted his head and he wagged his tail.

"The next commands are more difficult." She sat in the empty wheelchair she used for demonstrations, told Ranger to heel and rolled over to a card table that had been set up.

"Ranger, go in," she instructed. The dog glanced at her but didn't move.

"Ranger, go in," Erin repeated firmly. This time the black Lab went under the table, turned around and lay down facing her. His head was on his paws and his dark eyes watched her intently. She called him back out and praised him, then told him to jump on the table. This time Ranger obeyed immediately.

Freddie cheered, then stopped abruptly when Lucy put one finger to her lips.

Erin went through the procedure of telling Ranger to pick up a sock that was on the table, bring it to her and release it when she told him.

"As you work with your dogs, you'll develop customized commands and combinations for your own particular needs," she explained, getting up from the chair. She glanced at her watch as Nick came in the door and stood at the back of the room.

"We have another trip to the mall planned for tomorrow," she told the class. "Meanwhile, work with your dogs on what I've just showed you. I'll be around if you have any problems." She walked to the back of the room where Nick was standing.

"Would you go on the field trip with us in the morning and help out?" she asked as the familiar reaction to his presence hummed through her like an electric current. "We'll be short-handed again."

He shrugged. "Sure, as long as my boss doesn't need me to paint, pound or clip off parts of something." His tone was dry but his smile belied its seriousness.

"I'll see if I can get you excused for a while," Erin teased back, wondering if he thought he was spending too much time helping Darren. She would have liked to say more, to ask if he had been thinking about her as she had him. Whether the feelings that burned through her when they were close affected him, too, or if he was just looking for a diversion. Of course, she couldn't voice any of that. Instead, she thanked him and walked away, congratulating herself for concealing her own growing feelings.

Watching her go back to the students who had spread out in the large room and were working in pairs with their dogs, Nick recalled with excruciating detail how she had felt in his arms on that windy beach. His body clenched with tension at the memory and he turned toward the door before anyone could notice her effect on him.

Hard physical labor didn't help; cold showers were useless. Maybe what he needed was to give in to temptation and take her to bed. He didn't think she'd be unwilling, not the way she responded to his kisses. He drew his hands into hard fists as his breath hissed between his teeth. He leaned his head against the wall and swore silently.

That almost drove him over the edge, her response. God, how

he wanted her! Maybe one taste of the sweet passion that simmered between them, flaring up whenever they touched, would be enough.

His sharp bark of laughter was almost painful. Who was he kidding?

"Are you okay?" Anna had pushed open the door and was looking up at Nick. She was in her chair, as she usually was by this time of day if not earlier.

Nick had straightened abruptly when the door opened. Now he forced his fisted hands to relax and his facial muscles to smile.

"Yeah, I just have a little headache."

"I could get you some aspirin," she offered. "Or something else if that upsets your stomach."

Nick felt like a heel for lying to her. "No, thanks." He stepped back so she could come through the door. "I have something in my room."

"Okay." Anna's expression was still concerned. He hoped she wouldn't say anything to Erin. Or to Lucy. He didn't want his sister worrying about him.

"I'll see you later." He left without glancing back to see if Anna was watching. On the way to his unit, he realized that he really did have a headache and it was growing worse by the second.

"Where's Fred?" Erin asked, glancing around the open mall area. She had spoken with his parents in Spokane the evening before, telling them how well he was doing. His mom had wanted to stay with him at the center, but she was needed at home and his father had to work. They called frequently and were coming to visit the next weekend.

"He was here a minute ago," Ray said, glancing around.

Erin wasn't worried. Queenie was with him. "I'll go look."

"I'll go," Nick offered. He'd barely spoken to Erin during the outing, staying close to Lucy instead. For once, Erin hadn't had the energy to keep him from overdoing his watch-dog routine. Her personal feelings were becoming too involved for her to feel confident about her own objectivity.

"No, that's okay. I'll go," she replied, her gaze skimming over the plaid flannel shirt that outlined his broad shoulders and brought out the green of his eyes.

Earlier, she had caught herself staring when he bent to pick up some litter and toss it into a garbage can. His jeans had tightened across his buttocks and muscular thighs in a way that had her grinning like a lovesick fool and then glancing around hastily to see if anyone else noticed. Luckily, the others had been preoccupied with a crafts show set up in the middle of the mall.

Now Nick shrugged and turned back to his sister when she called his name insistently. Erin took advantage of his distraction to head toward the pet store. As soon as she rounded the corner onto the side branch of the mall, she saw Freddie and Queenie. They were surrounded by several older boys in disreputable clothing. From Freddie's expression, Erin didn't think their intentions were friendly.

"What do you say when you want to get by us, jerk?" one of the boys demanded as Erin got within hearing distance. His friends laughed raucously and Queenie, sensing their hostility, began to bark.

"Oh, tough dog," another of the boys said, lifting his booted foot as if to kick her.

"Leave her alone!" Freddie shouted. There were tears dribbling down his cheeks.

"That's enough!" Erin brushed past the boys to drop a reassuring hand on Freddie's shoulder.

"I'm sorry," he began in an agitated voice. "I wanted to see the fish and then they wouldn't—"

"It's okay," she told him, bending closer. "It's not your fault." When she straightened, she saw that Freddie's tormentors were older than she had first thought, and looked like what her mother would have called hoodlums.

"You should be ashamed," she ground out, staring down each of them in turn. "Haven't you got anything better to do than pick on someone smaller than you?"

"Aw, he's just a spaz," one of them said.

His companion, sporting hair that was shaved on the sides and long on the top and back, took a step closer. He had a silver crucifix hanging from one ear and a tattoo on his pockmarked cheek. He looked Erin up and down as he circled around behind her.

"This babe is more my speed, anyway," he said to the others as

Erin tried to stay between him and Freddie without turning her back.

"Hey, sweet thing, how'd you like to go out behind the mall and let me—"

Before he could complete his suggestion, Nick appeared abruptly and grabbed the front of his dirty tee-shirt in both hands. As the boy's voice broke off on a squeak of protest, Erin almost sagged with relief. Nick jerked him forward, so he was standing on tiptoe.

"I'd advise you to shut your mouth," Nick told him in a quiet voice that dripped with menace. The youth in his grip paled visibly as his companions began edging away.

"Nick," Erin cautioned, anxious not to make a scene. "It's okay. Let's just go."

"Knock it off, man. We didn't mean anything," Nick's captive whined.

"What's going on here?" Nick asked Erin.

"They were bothering Freddie, but he's okay now," she said, glancing at the little boy for confirmation.

"They were making fun of me," he said, voice more difficult to understand than usual. "And then Erin came."

Nick looked back at her while the young troublemaker struggled to get loose. "You okay?"

"Yes, I'm fine."

"Come on, man," the boy in Nick's grasp pleaded. "Let me go."

Erin felt nothing but disgust toward him. Still, she didn't want Freddie more upset than he already was and she could see that they were drawing a crowd of curious shoppers.

"Nick, please," she repeated. "Let's get out of here."

He glared at the punk.

"What's the problem here?" demanded a heavyset security guard as he hurried toward them, one hand holding a walkie-talkie and the other resting on the handle of a billy club stuck into his belt.

Nick immediately let go of the boy's shirt.

"No problem," he told the guard, forcing a smile. "Just a little misunderstanding."

"That's right," the boy agreed, face growing red.

"I told you before to stay out of here, you and your friends," the guard shouted. "Now, beat it. If I see you around here again,

I'm calling the cops." He watched, grim faced, while the three boys walked rapidly away.

Erin pulled on Nick's arm. "Come on." The others would be wondering where they'd gotten to.

He glanced at her and then at Freddie. "You okay, son?"

Freddie seemed fully recovered. He grinned up at Nick. "You should have heard Queenie," he said. "She growled and barked at them. If I let her, she would have torn them apart."

Nick turned his attention back to Erin. He looked relieved. "How about you?"

"I'm fine," she repeated. "Let's just get out of here."

The trio of boys disappeared out the exit and the guard riveted his gaze on Erin. "You want to file a complaint?" he asked. "We've had trouble with the three of them before."

She shook her head. "No, but thank you for coming so quickly. No harm done, I guess." She glanced around at the small crowd that had gathered and tried to smile reassuringly. "No problem."

The guard shrugged. "Okay." After Erin and Nick had both thanked him, he lumbered away, talking into the radio he held to his mouth.

Beside Erin, Nick radiated tension like a trained Doberman on patrol. She touched his arm. "Come on." She glanced at Freddie, who was already wheeling himself back in the direction from which Erin had come, the border collie at his side. He seemed to be over the unpleasant experience. As she started to follow them, Nick lightly touched her arm.

"Hey," he asked in a low voice, "are you really okay?"

Erin hesitated, taking a deep breath. The scene might have been much nastier if Nick hadn't arrived when he did.

"Thanks to you," she told him sincerely.

For a moment, they stood looking deep into each other's eyes. It felt good to be rescued. Especially by a man like Nick.

"I wanted to pound that punk into the floor," he growled. "Especially when I heard the way he was talking to you."

Erin's cheeks flamed at the reminder of what the boy had been saying. She had hoped that Nick hadn't heard. At least the kid hadn't had the opportunity to complete his lewd offer. She looked down at her feet, embarrassed.

"You got here just in time," she murmured.

Nick crooked one finger under her chin and lifted it gently. "In the nick of time?" he teased.

A chuckle escaped her lips. "I'd say so," she replied. "Thanks again."

His eyes darkened. He was standing close. "Anytime," he whispered, stroking his finger along her jaw. "For you, anytime."

Erin glanced around, relieved to see that no one was paying any attention to them. Swallowing, she said, "We'd better find the others, before Freddie has them convinced that Queenie fought off an entire army of assailants."

For a moment, Nick merely stared down at her. "Yeah," he drawled finally. "I guess we have to go back. I'd much rather buy you some coffee and let you tell me what a hero I am." Before Erin could formulate a reply, he grabbed her hand in his. For once, she didn't even want to pull it loose.

After dinner, Erin sought Nick out again to thank him for rescuing her and Freddie at the mall. The incident had been the main topic of conversation at dinner, but she hadn't had the chance to speak to Nick directly. He had left before she was done eating. When she went outside afterward, she heard the thunk of a basketball bouncing on the blacktop and walked around to where the hoop stood in a pool of light. Nick was there, playing alone.

"No more one on one," he gasped, leaping for the basket. "So don't even ask." The ball rimmed the hoop and went in. He lunged to snag it from the air. Sweat ran down his face despite the cool evening air.

"No," Erin agreed. "I don't think my ankle is ready for a game of one on one." He looked like a man pursued by devils. She wondered what, exactly, was on his mind. While she watched, he scooped up a towel and mopped his face.

"Don't let me interrupt you," she said, intending to leave him.

"It's okay," Nick mumbled from the confines of the towel. "I'm done." He dropped it and bent over, hands braced on his knees as he struggled to catch his breath. He'd pushed himself, hard, but it hadn't helped.

"You'll get chilled standing around out here," Erin said. "You'd better get a shower."

Nick couldn't help but grin at her bossy tone. "Do you have brothers?" he asked, sure neither she nor her parents had mentioned siblings.

"No." She looked puzzled. "Why?"

"You give orders like a little mother," he said, enjoying her obvious discomfort. "And I'm pretty sure you don't have any children."

"No, I don't." She sounded annoyed. "Makes no difference to me if you want to stand around and get pneumonia, I guess," she continued.

"Did you want to talk about something in particular?" he asked. Maybe she had just wanted to see him. To talk. To test the same demon hormones that tormented him whenever she was around. Hell, even when she wasn't.

He pushed his damp hair off his forehead. "How about I take a shower and then drop by?" he asked. "Will you be in your apartment?"

Erin flushed and he wondered what she was thinking. "No, I'll be in the office," she said. "But you don't need to bother."

He shook his head and grabbed the towel and ball. "No bother," he told her, walking quickly away before she could tell him not to come by at all.

Erin stared after him, trying to decide if she was pleased or annoyed at his insistence. A few notes of his almost tuneless whistling floated back to her and she smiled. Who was she kidding?

Erin was having trouble concentrating. She found herself staring at the computer screen without seeing it, her thoughts drifting. When the knock came at the door, she jumped even though she had been expecting it.

"Come in," she called, taking a deep breath. She stared hard at the screen, frowning with concentration. The words swam before her eyes.

"Hi."

She forced herself to turn slowly at the sound of Nick's voice. He had showered and his hair was damp. Several strands fell across his forehead; her fingers itched to push them back. He was wearing a sweatshirt and faded jeans, and a whiff of something that reminded her of dark forests and solitude teased her nostrils.

Erin swallowed. "Hi." She licked her suddenly dry lips, then flushed when she saw the way Nick was watching her mouth. Nervously, she tapped on a few computer keys to end the program on which she was working, and pushed her chair away from the desk. Rising, she went quickly to the supply cabinet to get another box of disks. The tiny hairs on the back of her neck warned her that Nick had moved nearer. When she turned, he trapped her against the wall, bracketing her with his arms, and leaned close.

Erin stared into his eyes. The attraction between them was so strong she could feel it pulsating, like a light show just beyond the periphery of her vision.

"Did you want me?" he asked in a husky whisper. One corner of his mouth quirked at the loaded question.

Helpless against his charm, she returned the grin. "I'm not sure how to answer that."

"Try the truth." The humor faded and his hooded eyes searched her face as if he were greedy for clues.

She glanced past him toward the window. The blinds were open and anyone walking by would see them.

"I, uh," she began and then faltered to a stop. Nick turned, following the line of her vision.

"Don't move," he commanded.

She watched him cross to the window and pull the blinds closed. Her heart thudded in tune with his footsteps as he came back. The idea of moving barely registered before he crowded close again.

"What are you doing?" she croaked as he eased his body up to hers so they were almost touching.

"Trying to seduce you," he murmured into her ear. "How'm I doing?"

There was humor in his voice as well as desire. For some reason, it relaxed her. She lifted her hands and let her fingers sink into his hair as he angled his head.

"You're doing fine," she whispered against his lips.

The kiss was sweet, sensual and throbbing with promise. She moved her mouth against his, hungry for more, and his hands tightened on her shoulders. She was barely aware of her fingers sifting through the heavy silk of his hair when the door burst abruptly open.

"Oops," Anna exclaimed as they sprang apart like guilty adolescents. Her face turned pink but her grin was unrepentant. "I'm sorry. I didn't know anyone was in here," she continued as Erin moved a couple of decorous feet away from Nick. "I saw the light on and thought I'd forgotten to turn it off." She wheeled her chair around. "Just go back to what you were doing," she added over her shoulder.

"Anna!" Erin exclaimed, and then stopped, not sure what else to say. It would be useless to try to deny what her partner had undoubtedly seen with her own eyes.

Anna merely lifted her hand in a token wave and kept going. "Later, dudes!"

Nick went to the door and shut it, then looked at Erin with a speculative expression.

"Is the mood shattered?" he asked with raised eyebrows, as he reached for her.

She stepped back, out of his reach. Every screaming nerve in her body wanted her to walk into his embrace and stay there. His arms dropped to his sides.

"I was afraid of that," he muttered wryly.

"I'm sorry." Erin folded her arms across her chest and looked away.

He sighed. "Well," he said, resigned, "what did you want to talk to me about?"

"Lucy," she said without hesitation. "I just wanted you to know how truly well she's doing. She's been working hard and I told her as much. She and Max are making great progress. I'm pleased."

Nick's expression remained impassive. His fingers traced an invisible pattern on the top of the desk while he stared at his hand as if he had never seen it before.

"I'm glad," he said after a moment of silence.

"Are you?" she questioned.

His head came up sharply. "What does that mean?"

"I've wondered," Erin found herself admitting. "You can't blame me when I know how you feel about this whole program." She made a sweeping gesture.

"I love my sister." Nick's voice was harsh.

"I know that." Erin spoke quickly, persuasive arguments dancing on her tongue. "But love can blind a person to what's best."

"What's best according to Erin McKenzie?" There was a sneer in his voice and his smile held no warmth. "You can't pretend to know what I feel when I see Lucy in that wheelchair."

His voice had risen sharply.

"Stop punishing yourself!" Erin shouted back. She made an effort at control. "It isn't helping her, and it sure as hell isn't helping you."

Nick blinked in surprise. He raked a hand through his damp hair, leaving it standing in unsteady spikes. "Damn, but you're stubborn," he said.

Incredulity roared through Erin and she stamped her foot. "How can *you* call *me* stubborn?" she sputtered, jamming her fisted hands onto her hips. "You hang onto your guilt like a security blanket!"

Nick's dark brows bunched into a thunderous frown and his cheeks darkened. "You don't know what you're talking about."

"Oh, Nick, I do," she moaned in a softer voice. "I've seen it before." She moved closer, clutching his arm, wanting to shake him but resisting. "It's crippling, more so than any accident or disease. Guilt will cripple you and it will do its best to keep Lucy a cripple, too."

He wrenched his arm loose, and his eyes flashed green fire. "Stay out of it," he snarled, glaring. "You don't understand how I feel." For a moment, his face was tortured. "No one does." Then his expression closed up as if he regretted revealing as much as he had. With one last, angry glance, he whirled and yanked open the door.

"Nick!" she exclaimed, trying to stop him.

He kept going, shutting the door with a gentleness that was somehow more ominous than if he had slammed it.

Erin sank into the steno chair and stared at the blank screen. How could she convince him? How could she even make him listen?

She put her elbows on the desk and rested her head on her hands. The only way to help Nick was to find a way to help Lucy first.

* * *

While Erin was contemplating the problem of Nick and his guilt, he paid Lucy and Max a visit.

"Come on in," she said, opening the door wider. She wore a smile of welcome.

"How are you?" he demanded, still fuming over his shouting match with Erin.

"I think the more appropriate question is, how are you?" She gestured toward the couch and Nick dropped onto the cushion.

When it came to Nick, Lucy's perception was always surprising. She could read him like a sundial on a bright day. He didn't know what to say, wasn't sure why he had even come by. Without making a conscious decision, he found himself telling his sister about the argument he had just had with Erin. He didn't mention the kiss and wasn't specific about what was said, but he did tell her that Erin was the most exasperating woman he had ever had the misfortune to run across.

"I knew it!" Lucy exclaimed when he was done, clapping her hands together. Beside her, Max rose to his feet, his eyes on his mistress.

"It's okay," she said, patting his head. "Max, down." With a noisy sigh, the dog settled himself beside her chair.

"Knew what?" Nick growled, frustrated. Lucy didn't have to look so pleased that Erin was driving him to distraction.

"You two are perfect for each other. I knew it the minute I saw you together." She looked so smug that exasperation exploded inside him.

"I didn't realize you'd been brain damaged," he snapped without thinking.

For a fraction of a second, Lucy looked as if he had slapped her. Then she tossed her head and smiled brightly.

"That's one of the few things that still works," she replied.

Nick rose and went to kneel beside her. "I'm sorry, peanut," he said, furious with himself. "That was a rotten thing to say and I wish to hell I could take it back." He bowed his head, regret eating into him like acid. Lucy was the last person in the world he wanted to hurt, the last one who deserved anything besides his love and support. And his undivided loyalty.

She stroked his head with her good hand while he silently berated himself.

"Is the truth that upsetting?" she asked, and he could hear the restored good humor in her voice.

Relief made him raise his head. Hesitantly, he returned her teasing smile. "What truth?"

Lucy's voice brimmed with satisfaction. "You've fallen for Erin," she pronounced.

Eight

Nick was dumbfounded by Lucy's pronouncement that he had fallen for Erin. Perhaps he wanted the provocative redhead, but that didn't mean that he was emotionally involved. Ignoring the tiny voice that tried to tell him his interest in her didn't entirely originate below the waist, he jumped to his feet.

"That's absurd!"

Lucy's grin widened, infuriating him. Before more angry words could erupt without his permission, he bit down hard on his surging temper and forced himself to adopt a wry grin.

"I don't know where you get some of your ideas," he said, shaking his head. "I admit that Erin's a beautiful woman—"

"Ah. You admit you've noticed," Lucy cut in with a cheeky look.

"Sister, dear, I'm not dead," he drawled. "But I don't fall for every attractive woman I meet."

"I didn't say that," Lucy protested. "But Erin—"

It was his turn to interrupt. "—runs this service center," he finished for her.

"I was talking to Anna the other day," Lucy said, switching topics so fast that Nick blinked in temporary confusion.

"Oh?"

"She told me that she and Erin met in college."

Nick nodded his agreement. He knew that, too. "That's when Anna's MS was diagnosed," he said.

"I know. But she met Darren after that." Lucy paused expectantly.

Nick's brows rose in surprise. Had Anna told Darren about her condition before they got involved? That would have been tough, for both of them.

"They fell in love and got married, even though Darren knew she was going to get worse," Lucy continued. "Isn't that romantic?"

"It would be hard to deal with," Nick said. Lucy might see it as romantic, but he knew how so many different elements could put a strain on a relationship. Romantic wasn't the word he would have used to describe the situation they must have found themselves in. Still, he hesitated to tell his sister that.

Lucy's eyes filled with sudden tears. "Don't you get it?" she demanded, voice shaky.

An icy chill went through Nick. He rose and bent over her, taking her hand in his. "What is it, baby? What's upsetting you?"

Lucy brushed the tears away awkwardly. "If Anna could find someone to love her, maybe I can, too," she said, her smile wobbly around the edges. "I am going to have a life, and I'm going to be happy."

"Of course you are," Nick agreed, squeezing her hand. "Of course you are." Silently, he couldn't help but wonder if either of them would ever find real happiness again.

Later that evening, Nick still wondered if Lucy was deluding herself. If so, she was heading for a fall. It was Erin's fault for giving her false hopes, for promising her that a companion dog would be a miracle cure.

He needed to talk to Erin, and he didn't feel like waiting until the next morning when there would be no opportunity to get her alone. Before he could have second thoughts, he went over and knocked on the door of her apartment.

When Erin opened the door, Anna was behind her.

"Hi," Erin said. "Come on in."

He glanced at Anna and felt the slow heat of embarrassment spreading across his face. He wondered what the two women had been discussing. The kiss that Anna had interrupted? He forced himself to meet her eyes and ignore the amusement he was sure twinkled there.

"Anna," he greeted her gravely. "How are you?"

"Fine, thanks." Her answering smile was bland but he still regarded her warily. Had she told Darren? Not that the other man would mention it to Nick. He had learned after working side by side with Anna's husband that he was remarkably easy-going. And he didn't pry. He wouldn't avail himself of the chance to give Nick a hard time, but would probably be a good listener if Nick chose to bring up the incident himself. Not that he would! His own emotions were still too confused. His feelings toward Erin grew stronger each day, even though he knew it was a no-win situation for both of them.

"Well," Erin said as the silence began to stretch uncomfortably, "I guess I'll see you tomorrow, Anna."

Her friend glanced up and Erin hoped she wouldn't say anything to reveal what they had been talking about. Anna had said her only interest was that Erin not get hurt, but Erin wasn't ready to discuss her feelings for Nick, wasn't even ready to deal with them herself.

"Sure thing." Anna wheeled out the door, giving Nick a wave as she did. "Good night, you two."

" 'Night," Nick replied.

Erin wondered what he wanted. Wondered if he would kiss her again, and found that the idea made her feel both fuzzy-warm with longing and brittle with tension. If he did kiss her, what would she do? Resist the urgent pull she felt toward him or give in to it?

Maybe she should ask him to leave. No, one look at his handsome, troubled face and she knew she could no more turn him away than she could turn her back on a client who desperately needed a dog.

Erin opened the door wider as he stood hesitantly on the threshold. His grin was slightly crooked as he brushed past her and she shut it behind him.

"I'm sorry I came by so late."

"It's okay. What can I do for you?" Erin asked, trying to stay cool and calm when part of her wanted to grab him. The image of his startled reaction had her turning a chuckle into a discreet cough.

Now that Nick was alone with her, he was having a tough time keeping his mind on why he was there. She was wearing an aqua blue sweater in a cuddly knit that hinted at her womanly shape, along with her inevitable faded, snug jeans. Little silver cowboy boots set with turquoise stones gleamed in her ears. Her short hair was in its usual fiery disarray, reminding him of a vivid marigold blossom, and her eyes were wide with curiosity. Color bloomed on her normally creamy cheeks and he wondered if she was as nervous as he was.

He glanced away, studying the picture of two wolves in the snow on her wall, and raked a hand through his hair. The flowery scent he had come to associate with Erin filled his head and the room was so quiet he imagined he could hear her breathing.

Nick looked into her upturned face and something broke loose inside him. He moved forward hesitantly and reached out to her.

"I couldn't stay away," he confessed, putting his hands on her shoulders. Her bones felt delicate beneath his touch. She tensed and he heard her sharp intake of breath, but her gaze was steady. It never wavered as he lowered his head.

Erin slid her arms around his waist and met the kiss halfway. For a timeless moment, she savored the feel of him. Her reservations fled. Then, too soon, she felt his hands pushing gently on her shoulders. His eyes, when she could again focus, were hooded, revealing nothing.

"I shouldn't have done that."

"Then why did you?" she demanded, crossing her arms over her breasts protectively.

He looked at the couch. "May I?"

At her jerky nod, he sat down and threw one arm along the back. Erin sank into a chair across from him, glad to get off legs that had begun to tremble. Impatient, she waited for him to speak.

"You're giving Lucy false hopes," he said baldly.

Erin had been about to relax into the chair. At his words, she straightened, her fingers digging into the padded arms.

"How so?"

His expression was troubled. "She's been talking to Anna and now she feels that anything is possible, even marriage, from what I can tell."

"How's that my fault?"

"It's the dogs," he said. "She thinks that anything is possible as long as she has one of your dogs."

Erin couldn't help but smile. "Within reason, it is."

He leaned back and shut his eyes. His forehead was creased. "Let's be serious here."

"I am being serious," Erin replied, trying to hang onto her patience. "It happens all the time. Look at Anna and Darren. They're very happy."

Nick made a dismissive gesture. "I'm sure they're the exception," he said.

Erin could have throttled him. "Do you always discount anything that doesn't back up your own narrow view of the world?" she asked, temper slipping a notch.

He narrowed his eyes. "Do you always look at things through rose-colored glasses?"

Too agitated to remain seated, Erin leaped to her feet. Nick did the same, but she refused to let him intimidate her.

"I think that you're the one without hope," she said quietly. "I don't know what made you so pessimistic, but I'm getting a little tired of your doom-and-gloom attitude."

She saw the anger flare in his eyes. "And I'm getting tired of your Mary Poppins act."

She almost laughed. "Mary Poppins!" The image of Julie Andrews flying across the screen as she gripped her umbrella flashed before Erin's eyes.

"That's right," he growled.

Erin couldn't suppress a grin. The image was just too comical. To her surprise, an answering grin flashed across Nick's face. Then he sobered.

Before he could speak, she grasped his hand and pulled him back down on the couch. "Tell me about the accident," she invited in a gentler tone. Perhaps talking about it would exorcise some of his guilt.

He sighed noisily and rested his head against the back of the couch. "I try not to think about it."

"It would do you good to talk about what happened," she insisted. "Have you ever really discussed it with anyone?" Surely his family had supported him, tried to reassure him that the accident hadn't been his fault. Lucy insisted it wasn't.

To her surprise, he shook his head. "No, I guess not. My father isn't a man who goes on about his feelings, or pries into anyone else's. Lucy's always been Mom's baby. How could I make her feel any worse than she already did by reminding her?"

"I can understand that," Erin reassured him, "But I'd like to hear about it. If you want to tell me." She held her breath, waiting for his angry explosion demanding that she mind her own business.

It never came. Instead, Nick leaned forward. He folded her hand in one of his and bowed his head. Erin barely resisted the urge to smooth back his hair.

"We were arguing," he said after a long pause. "Lucy wanted to take an expensive modeling course." His voice was bitter and Erin knew the bitterness was turned against himself.

"She'd quit college because she wanted to learn about hair and make up. Then she quit beauty school when she found out there was more to it than that." He fell silent.

Beside him, Erin squeezed his hand. "You don't sound so unreasonable," she said.

He raised her hand to his mouth and kissed it.

"Thanks, but somehow the cost of a modeling course doesn't seem so important now." After a moment, he continued. "Anyway, I wasn't paying much attention to the traffic. We were sitting at a light. When it turned green, I started to go. A drunk ran the light. He was speeding when he hit Lucy's side of the car. She never had a chance."

"It doesn't sound like there was anything you could have—"

"I could have been paying attention," Nick cut in angrily. "I could have looked before I started across that intersection. Instead, I was too angry about spending a few hundred bucks to bother!"

Erin slid closer and grasped his bare forearm with her free hand. "Things like that happen," she told him. "If you hadn't been arguing, it probably would have still happened. Only you wouldn't feel so guilty." She rubbed his arm, trying to comfort him. "Come on," she urged. "It's time to let go. It wasn't your fault."

Nick raised his bowed head and met her gaze. His eyes darkened. The slow change in the atmosphere between them made Erin begin to nibble at her lower lip. Why did desire always get in the way when it came to the two of them?

She let go of his arm. He tightened his hold on her other hand. "Thanks," he said in a low voice. "I know what you're trying to do."

"So," she said, trying to lighten the atmosphere between them, "how'm I doing?"

His eyes glinted with awareness at her use of the same phrasing he had when he admitted trying to seduce her. Then his attention dropped to her mouth.

"I'm not sure what's going on here, but I'm damn tired of fighting it," he breathed.

Erin couldn't have agreed more. However this thing between them ended, and she was pretty sure it was going to end badly, she wanted everything he was willing to give her before it did.

She smiled. As if he had been waiting for a sign, he swooped like a bird of prey and covered her mouth in a kiss that began tenderly—and then exploded in a conflagration of need.

After a few heated moments, he sucked in a ragged breath and lifted his head.

"If you've got any second thoughts," he said thickly, "you'd better stop me now. Otherwise I can't promise to let you go."

Erin touched his cheek with her fingers. Then she rose, more sure of what she was about to do than she had been about anything in a long time. She reached out her hand.

Nick grasped her fingers and got to his feet, expression puzzled.

"My bedroom is this way," she said, leading him down the short hallway.

He tugged on her arm, stopping her. Then, as pleasure swept through her, he scooped her into his arms. She clasped his neck as they kissed again, tenderly.

"I'll make it special for you," he murmured, his voice husky with emotion. "This is going to be something neither of us will ever forget."

Nick dropped her gently on the bed and followed her down, unwrapping her body like a very special present and stopping to kiss and caress each new part of her he uncovered. On a sigh of need, Erin banished the last words he had spoken, words that already sounded like a sad good-bye, and gave herself up to his tender yet passionate attention.

Although his breathing was rough and his body trembled with need, she could tell that he was determined to take it slow. Flames of pleasure licked at her like fiery tongues as his hands swept over her and he murmured his approval. Needs spiraled within her. She reached for his shirt, fumbled with the buttons and waited impa-

tiently as he sat up to shrug his way out of it. When her eager
fingers reached for the fastening of his jeans, he caught her hands
in his.

"One accidental touch from you and the speed of this whole
scenario is going into triple time," he rasped. "I'd better finish this
myself."

Erin struggled to free her hands. Her control was shaky and she
wanted to push him much nearer the end of his. At his first touch,
she had started to burn. Next time, if there was a next time, they
could wander from kiss to tender, aching kiss. But this time she
wanted him, all the way, as soon as he could bury himself inside
her.

"What is it?" he asked as she pulled loose from his grasp. "Have
you changed your mind?"

She almost laughed. Instead of answering him, she tore free the
snap of his jeans.

"Erin," he gasped. "What are you doing?"

She touched the bare skin of his stomach. It was hot to her touch.
His muscles quivered. Her fingers slid into his open jeans, tangled
in the coarse hair and then slipped lower still. His answering groan
was raw, guttural. Then he rolled off the bed. He pulled out his
wallet and took something from it. Dropping the wallet to the floor,
he shucked off his jeans and briefs while Erin stared.

Dazzled by the sight of him, she forgot all about asking why he
had obviously come prepared. He tore open the foil packet and
turned away for a moment. She reached out her arms, eager for
his possession. He kissed her hard, thrusting his tongue into her
mouth as he covered her body with his and opened her legs with
his knee. His gaze never wavered as he filled her.

Erin wrapped her legs around his lean hips, welcoming him as
he went still, buried deep inside her.

Her arms tightened. With a shuddering sigh, he began to move.
She was with him every step of the way, arching to meet each
thrust, until he drove her over the edge. Then she heard his deep
cry and knew that he followed her, even as she soared. Time hung
suspended as they found heaven together.

Twice more as she lay beside him in the darkness, he wakened
her with greedy hands. First came the slow, tender loving they had
each imagined, followed by a heated clash of need and want and

greed that had them crying out together and then collapsing into exhausted slumber—tangled close and holding tight as if both were afraid letting go might be forever.

"Did Nick oversleep?" Erin asked Lucy at breakfast the next morning when he failed to appear.

Lucy's eyes, so like his, widened with surprise. "Didn't he say anything to you?"

"About what?" Erin hoped that no evidence of the tumultuous night she and Nick had shared lingered in her expression. She had wakened alone, regretting the need for propriety that had no doubt sent him back to his own unit in the dawn hours while she slept, exhausted from his expert ministrations. Now she dreaded seeing him again in front of an audience, but still couldn't keep her eyes from darting to the door each time it opened.

"Tell me about what?" she repeated when Lucy didn't immediately reply.

"I thought he'd say something before he left."

An icy chill ran down Erin's spine. "Left for where?" she demanded.

Lucy's eyes stayed on her plate. "Nick's gone back to Eugene."

Nine

Erin could almost feel the blood draining from her face. She swallowed, trying to maintain some shred of composure. All she could think about was that Nick had left. Had bedded her and left without a word. Without a backward glance!

"No," she managed to answer Lucy. "He didn't say anything to me." She hated the other girl's sympathetic expression, hated having everyone hear the awkward exchange.

"Apparently there were some things at the company that needed his immediate attention," Lucy said. "He said he'd probably be back in a couple of days."

Relief flooded Erin. He wasn't gone for good. Then she realized that he had still been able to walk away after what they had shared.

Obviously, it had meant something different to Nick than it had to her. Something less.

She studied the eggs congealing on her plate. One bite would gag her; she knew it as surely as she knew her name. Still, she went through the motions of cutting up the food and moving it around.

"Is anything wrong?" Anna asked quietly.

Erin pinned on a smile and shook her head. "No. As long as Lucy's okay, everything's fine." She doubted Anna believed her, but knew her friend wouldn't question her further. Not right now, anyway.

"I'm fine," Lucy said. "It's kind of a relief to be out from under Nick's microscope for a little while."

"He means well," Erin defended.

Beside her, Jane chuckled. "I know all about watchful relatives," she said. "My sister still won't believe I can manage by myself. Took her months after I got my first dog to stop checking on me every day."

The conversation around Erin moved on to more ordinary things, plans after graduation, family that was missed. Without looking at Anna, she nibbled at a piece of toast and sipped her coffee. And decided she was more angry than hurt.

What had Nick thought she was going to do, have her father chase him with a shotgun? She was a big girl; she knew he wasn't looking for anything permanent. Neither was she. Was she?

She never had asked him why he'd had those condoms in his wallet, either. Let alone demanded to know his intentions. But then, she was no more ready for complications to her life than he was!

So why had he run?

Maybe his father *had* called about some crisis. Maybe Nick hadn't wanted to wake her. Erin knew she was clutching at straws. She dropped the toast she had been crumbling onto her plate and wiped her fingers.

Maybe after he had satisfied his curiosity or assuaged his hormones, Nick had no further use for her, but she couldn't quite convince herself that he was capable of that kind of calculation. Dammit, she'd been there—wrapped up with him. What they had shared was more than just sex and hormones.

She glanced around, but no one at the long table paid any attention to her. Even Anna was deep in conversation with Darren. Erin rose and dumped her tray. Then she headed outside. The weather matched her mood. The sky was leaden, the rain pouring down in a near-solid curtain. Working one of the dogs in the covered area would calm her; it always had in the past.

Nick pulled into the parking lot behind the office of Blackwood Construction, glad to see that his father's pickup was still there. Nick hadn't called before he left. It had been too early. Instead, he had started at dawn and driven almost straight through with one stop for coffee and gas. Now his stomach rumbled as he bounded up the steps to the front door, but he ignored it. Maybe some penance would be good for him. Leaving Monroe, and Erin, the way he had was pretty shabby. He should call, but he just wasn't ready to talk to her.

"Hi, Dad," he said, as he went in the front door. His father was standing over the bookkeeper's desk holding a computer printout.

"Nick! How are you?" He crossed the room and stuck out his hand.

"Fine," Nick replied, shaking it before greeting Ruby, the bookkeeper.

"I didn't expect to see you today," his father said, preceding Nick into the office they shared.

Nick shrugged. "I saw an opportunity to come back and I took it."

His father glanced at his watch. "You must have left there pretty early. How's Lucy?"

Nick hesitated, not wanting to worry him. "She's still in the program," he said at last. "I think she's doing well, but she has high hopes. Perhaps too high."

His father frowned and then he sat down behind the desk. "Let me bring you up to speed on the Highland Mall project first," he said. For the next half hour, they talked business. Then Nick's stomach rumbled again.

"I'd better give Mom a call, and then I've got to get something to eat," he said. "Do you have time for lunch?"

They ate while they discussed potential problem areas and, as soon as they were finished, they spent the afternoon visiting job sites.

Nick had hoped to drive back to Monroe the next morning; he wanted to see Erin and get things straightened out between them. Now it looked as if he was going to be stuck in Eugene for at least one more day.

Erin was having trouble concentrating on work. Nick had been gone since the day before and she was still angry. But she missed him, too, and wanted to find out why he had felt the need to escape. Despite what Lucy had said, Erin was still worried that he wouldn't come back at all.

She was taking advantage of a few free moments after lunch to read the newspaper when she happened to flip through a colorful ad brochure for a local department store chain. Erin glanced at one picture, started to move on and then went back to it. Her eyes widened as she studied the three attractive young women modeling casual separates.

Grabbing the phone book, Erin called the flagship store in downtown Seattle and finally tracked down the name of the agency that had produced the sales brochure. In a few more minutes, Erin was talking with the woman who had set up the shoot. They made an appointment for the next morning; Darren and Anna could take over the class for a few hours. Surprised at how smoothly everything had fallen into place, Erin hurried out of the office, eager to discuss what she had done with Lucy.

Lucy's eyes widened at the picture of the model in a wheelchair that Erin showed her.

"It's a new idea they're trying out, portraying real, everyday people," Erin told her. "The woman I talked to, Nita Blue, said they've gotten a tremendous public response to the ads and they're looking for more models like the one in the picture. I told her about you and she wants to see you."

"When?" Lucy asked.

"Tomorrow morning."

"Tomorrow?" Lucy gasped, grabbing at the ends of her hair. "I don't know. I need a trim. How would I get to the appointment? Maybe I should wait until I'm done here. I need to get ready first." She frowned, biting her lower lip.

"Don't worry," Erin told her. "You look great. The appointment is in downtown Seattle. I'll drive you and we'll take Max. It will be great experience for both of you."

Lucy hesitated and Erin was afraid she would refuse. Then her face cleared. "Why not?" she asked, raising her chin. "Won't Nick have a fit?"

Nick hadn't expected the welcome mat to be out when he got back from Eugene the next afternoon, but neither had he thought that both Lucy and Erin would be gone.

"Just where did you say they went?" he asked Anna, whom he had found working in the office after looking in on the class.

Anna smiled and shrugged. "They went somewhere together," she said unhelpfully. "Seattle, I think Erin said."

Nick could have throttled her. "But you don't know where? Or why?"

Anna glanced up again and then back to the computer screen. "I'm afraid I wasn't paying much attention."

Nick growled a thank you and stalked out. Anna knew more than she was saying, he was sure of it. What the hell was going on, anyway? He wondered if Darren would tell him and then dismissed the idea. He didn't want to interrupt the class again.

Nick was walking through the parking area in the drizzling rain, wondering what to do with himself, when the missing van pulled in. Erin was behind the wheel and Lucy was beside her.

He waited, hands jammed into his jacket pocket, while they got out. Max was with them.

Erin greeted him, cheeks pink, and his hands itched to pull her into his arms. He hadn't realized just how much he had missed her.

"Nick!" Lucy exclaimed. He could barely tear his gaze away from Erin. He bent to give Lucy a hug.

"Hi, baby." She looked different somehow, even prettier than usual, but he couldn't tell why. "Did you get your hair cut?" he asked.

Lucy laughed. She and Erin exchanged amused glances while Nick tried to gauge Erin's mood and failed utterly.

"No, I didn't get my hair cut," Lucy told him. "You could say I had a make over."

He had no idea what she was talking about.

"When did you get back?" she demanded. "And how are Mom and Dad?"

"I got back a little while ago," Nick told her. "Mom and Dad sent their love. They'll see you at graduation. Now, where have you and Erin been?"

Lucy took a deep breath and Nick felt a shiver of foreboding. She grabbed his hand and her grip was surprisingly strong.

"I'm so excited," she gushed. "I've been to a modeling agency! They took some test photos today and they might be interested in hiring me."

Nick couldn't have been more surprised if she had told him she'd been auditioning for the Northwest Ballet Company. He looked to Erin for an explanation.

"That's right." Her smile was slightly defiant. "Lucy just may fulfill that dream of hers after all."

For once, Nick was speechless.

Lucy didn't seem to expect a comment. "I want to get Max back to my apartment," she told Erin. "I don't think he feels too hot."

"Good idea."

Nick glanced at the dog, who stood at Lucy's side, tongue hanging out. "What's wrong with Max?"

"I think he might have a temperature," Erin said. "He just didn't act like himself today. I'm going to call the vet and see if she'd come over and check him out."

Lucy gave Nick's hand another squeeze before letting go. "We can talk more later."

He watched her roll away. He still had plenty of questions about her startling announcement. How could she be a fashion model in her condition? His concern for her was temporarily sidetracked when he realized that Erin was still standing beside him.

When he looked at her, she was regarding him with a wary expression.

"I missed you," he said, tempted to haul her into his arms and kiss her right there.

"Did you?"

He guessed he deserved that. "We need to talk," he told her. The first thing he had to do was apologize for leaving without saying good-bye, but the second was discovering whether kissing her could possibly be as good as he remembered.

"Let's go to my apartment where we won't be interrupted." Erin was relieved that Nick was back and would have liked nothing better than to spend the hours until the next morning the same way they had only three nights ago. But Nick was right. First, they had to talk.

Erin opened the door to her apartment and bent to pet her cat, who flipped over and presented his tummy for scratching.

"He's easy," Nick said.

Erin stiffened, wondering if he thought that she was easy, too.

"Would you like something to drink?" she asked. "I've got some orange soda in the fridge."

"No, thanks." He looked uncomfortable, and her heart sank. She didn't want him feeling awkward or guilty around her. The man carried enough guilt!

"Why don't you sit down while I give the vet a call," she said, picking up the phone. "I'll just be a moment."

As soon as she was done, she joined Nick on the couch, leaving a couple of feet between them.

"She'll be over late this afternoon." Erin felt the tension radiating from Nick, but wasn't sure how to dispel it.

"That's good. I hope that Max will be okay." Nick's expression was somber, his eyes dark and hooded as he stretched one arm across the back of the couch and regarded Erin silently. She would have given a lot to know what he was thinking.

"You wanted to talk," she coaxed as the silence became unbearable. It was difficult not to fidget when he was watching her so intently.

"I'm sorry," Nick said, startling her. "I never should have left the way I did."

"So, why did you?" she asked, idly twisting the gold chain bracelet her folks had given her for her last birthday.

Nick sighed and broke eye contact. Shiftless jumped onto his lap and began to knead his thigh with its front paws. Nick stroked the cat's fluffy fur absently.

"Push him down if you want," Erin said. If Nick told her that what had happened between them was a mistake, she was determined not to cry. At least, not in front of him.

"The cat's okay." After a moment, Shiftless jumped back off Nick's lap and headed to the tiny kitchen.

"I don't know what got into me," Nick began in a low voice. His gaze never wavered from hers. "I wanted you so much. I tried to fight it but it was no good." His smile was crooked and a lock of hair hung down on his forehead. "Being with you—" Nick closed his eyes and curled his hands into fists. "—it was so damn good, even better than I expected."

Erin remained silent, struggling to understand whatever point he was trying to make.

"Since the accident, I've done my best to put my needs aside," Nick continued. "I told myself that I owed Lucy that much. And I do," he added quickly. "But then, when I was with you, I didn't even remember that she existed. All I could think about was the way you made me feel." He slid over, closing the gap between them on the couch, and took her hand.

Erin swallowed the lump in her throat. Poor Nick, torturing himself over something he couldn't have helped.

"I guess I panicked," he said. "I'm sorry I lit out like I did. I hope you'll forgive me." There was a question in his eyes.

Erin took a deep breath, grateful he'd come back, determined to enjoy whatever he could give her, for as long as it lasted. Deliberately, she closed her mind off from thoughts of the future.

"I was hurt when Lucy told me you left," she admitted, "but I guess I understand." She raised her free hand and laid it along his cheek. "I missed you, too," she whispered.

"Sweetheart!" Nick exclaimed, pulling her into his arms. "I don't deserve your understanding, but I'll take it." His hold on her tightened and he kissed her thoroughly, leaving Erin with no doubts that he'd missed her. She clung to him, trying to reassure him with her lips and her touch. After a moment that went by too fast, he set her away from him.

"I wish we could stay here together until tomorrow morning," he confessed, voice rough with longing. "But someone would be bound to notice you were missing and come look for you."

Erin leaned forward to give him another quick kiss. His hands tightened on her upper arms and he prolonged the contact until her heart was beating in double time.

"I'd better tell Lucy when the vet's coming."

At the mention of Lucy's name, Nick remembered her trip to Seattle with Erin.

"I'll give her the message," he said. "I need to talk to her anyway."

If Erin had misgivings, she didn't voice them. "Okay," she said instead. "I'd better check on the class and see if Darren wants me to take over."

She got to her feet and so did Nick. He had a hundred questions about that morning, but didn't want to rock the newfound peace between the two of them. Lucy would tell him what he wanted to know.

"Do you have plans for this evening?" he asked.

Erin shook her head.

"Well, let's get away from here after supper," he suggested.

"I'd like that."

"We'll talk about it later, okay?" If he didn't get out of there, he was going to throw all his good intentions to the wind and carry her back into the bedroom. She must have read something of what he was feeling in his expression, because she walked him to the door and went out with him.

"I'll see you later," she said. The rain had stopped and the sky was lighter.

"Count on it." Nick stared intently, then turned away and headed toward his sister's.

"How's Max?" he asked when Lucy let him in.

She glanced toward where the dog was lying on the floor with his head on his paws. "About the same. Listless."

"Erin called the vet. She'll be over later this afternoon."

"Good." Lucy looked slightly more relieved. Nick had an idea what the dog had come to mean to her, and he didn't like it one bit. No animal could live up to the expectations that Erin had encouraged in Lucy and the others.

He felt bad asking her about that morning when she was concerned about Max. On the other hand, maybe getting her mind off the dog would help. "Tell me about this modeling business," he said, sitting down so he could look into her face.

"It was super," Lucy began. "Erin saw an ad in the newspaper, with models in wheelchairs."

This surprised Nick. He'd never heard of it before.

"She called around and found the agency that shot the ad," Lucy went on, "and she talked to the woman who set up the shoot. Erin told her about me and she wanted to see me, to find out if the camera likes me." A grin flashed across Lucy's face. "Wasn't that great of Erin to go to all that trouble?"

Nick made a non-committal answer. Better if Erin had discussed it with him, first. Then he remembered that he hadn't been around. Well, hell. She could have waited.

"Anyway," Lucy went on, scarcely drawing a breath, "they made me up and took a lot of test photos today. Nita, that's the woman at the agency, Nita Blue, said she thought they looked good, but wouldn't be sure until she studies them all. If I have promise, she's going to call me."

"Then what?" Nick asked brusquely. "How are you supposed to conduct a modeling career from two hundred miles away?"

Lucy's eyes widened at his question. "I'll get an apartment in Seattle," she said.

He snorted with disbelief and leaped to his feet. This was the kind of pipe dream Erin was encouraging! Didn't she realize how vulnerable Lucy was? How open to the most unrealistic ideas? The news from the agency was bound to be disappointing. Even if they did encourage Lucy, how could she possibly cope, alone in a strange city? Even Erin would be an hour's drive away, and busy with her own responsibilities.

Maybe the woman at the agency would let Lucy down easy and Nick would never have to voice his own doubts.

"It sounds like something, all right," he said vaguely. "Be sure to let me know the minute you hear."

"I will," Lucy replied with a lighthearted laugh that tore at him like claws. She hadn't laughed much in the last two years. "You can bet on it."

Nick glanced around. "I hope the vet has good news about Max."

For a moment, Lucy's eyes lost their sparkle. "Me, too."

* * *

Nick was surprised when Anna interrupted class late the next afternoon to summon Lucy to the office for a phone call. The sky had been threatening rain all day, but so far the promised storm had held off. Nick knew that Max was back in Lucy's apartment. The vet had prescribed an antibiotic and a couple of day's rest. Lucy had been sitting in on the class session without him.

Now he watched his sister as she followed Anna from the room, her cheeks flushed with excitement. She glanced over at Nick and gave him a thumbs-up sign before exiting the classroom. He could spot her underlying tension, and his heart ached for her. After she left, he glared accusingly at Erin, whose sober gaze met his own. Then he straightened abruptly from the wall he'd been leaning against and hurried after his sister. She was probably going to need him if this was the long-awaited call from the agency. And he was determined always to be there when Lucy needed him.

Nick hovered outside the office, as anxious as a prospective father outside the delivery room, watching her through the window and trying to read the parade of expressions that crossed her face. The news didn't appear to be bad. He wondered if this agency could be a front for some scheme to bilk handicapped people of their money.

Finally, Lucy nodded vigorously, said something more and replaced the receiver. Then, as he watched, she whirled her chair around and gave Anna a hug.

Confused, Nick was about to wrench open the office door when Lucy came barreling out to meet him.

"They loved the photos," she cried, clutching at him excitedly. "And they want to see me again as soon as I'm done here."

Nick had hoped she would realize the utter futility of trying to pull off a modeling career or anything else so far away from home and the people who loved her. Now it looked like it was up to him to talk sense to her.

He squatted down so they were at eye level. "It's a lovely dream," he began, taking Lucy's hand.

"A dream!" She backed up her chair as she pulled away from his grasp. "What are you trying to tell me?"

"Listen, babe—"

"It's no dream," she argued. "It's something I want to do. Something maybe I *can* do." Her eyes pleaded for understanding.

He hated to be the one to disillusion her. He glanced around but there was no one else in sight. Anna was still in the office. "Let's go back to your unit and see how Max is doing," he suggested. "We can talk there."

"We can talk here," Lucy contradicted. "Rather, I can talk and you can listen. I'm not the helpless cripple you're determined to keep me, Nick. And I resent the fact that you have no faith in me."

Her accusation came as a shock. He started to protest but she cut him off. "You see taking care of me as a way to deal with your guilt." Her perception surprised him. "But you don't have to feel guilty," she insisted. "It was an accident." Tears overflowed her eyes and ran down her cheeks.

Nick had to swallow the lump in his own throat. He blinked away the sudden moisture that blurred his vision.

"It's more than appeasing my guilt, as you call it," he argued when he could speak. "I'm trying to spare you from hurt and disappointment."

Lucy's tears came faster, increasing his pain for her. "You just don't think I have what it takes," she wailed. "You don't think I'm pretty enough, or tough enough, or bright enough to make it. And you don't think I'll stick to it, because I gave up on so many different things before."

Nick wanted to deny what she had said, but couldn't. He did think she would quit, just the way she had quit everything else when it got hard and wasn't any more fun.

"That isn't true!" he protested, but he knew his words were too late. Before he could add anything else, Lucy spun away and began wheeling toward her apartment. "I've changed," she yelled over her shoulder. "And not just physically, either. But you don't want to see it."

"Lucy!" He had to make her listen.

"Just leave me alone." She kept on going.

He made a move to follow and then hesitated. Perhaps they both needed a cooling off period first. He'd try again later.

"What did they say?" Erin demanded, rushing up to where he stood staring after Lucy. "Was it good news?"

"Depends on your point of view," Nick told her bitterly. "As far as I'm concerned, it only prolongs the hurt."

"What do you mean? Do they want to see her again or not?"

"Yeah, they say they do," Nick admitted. "But how do you know it's not some scam to get her money for expensive photographs or something else?"

Erin looked shocked. "It's a very reputable agency," she said. "I checked."

Nick should have known she would have looked into it. "Well, you already know how I feel," he said lamely.

"Yes, I do." Erin's eyes sparkled with defiance. "And I suppose you told Lucy just that."

He wasn't used to having to justify his actions. "That's right, I did. And I wish you'd stop interfering in her life," he added. "She needs some time alone right now to think things through."

Erin glanced in the direction in which his sister had disappeared. "I'm not the one who's trying to run her life," she pointed out. "I'm only trying to help her find a way to make her own choices."

"I'm her brother."

Erin appeared to consider what he'd said. She couldn't argue that. "Well," she continued hesitantly, "I guess I should get back to class anyway. I suppose I'll see her at dinner." Her troubled gaze settled on Nick. "I wish you felt differently," she said before she turned and hurried away.

I wish I could, Nick thought to himself, watching her go. And I wish our disagreements about Lucy didn't keep the two of us apart.

After the evening meal in the dining room, during which Lucy didn't make an appearance, Erin covered a plate of food and took it over to her apartment. The evening had delivered what the day had threatened. The temperature had plummeted and an icy rain shimmered in the outside lights. Erin was glad she didn't have to go anywhere that evening. Driving would be treacherous.

She knocked on Lucy's door. Max barked, but Erin didn't hear any other sounds and the door remained closed. She knocked again, then opened the door slowly. Max greeted her with a couple of thumps of his tail. Perhaps Lucy was asleep.

Erin patted the dog's head. "Feeling better, boy?" she asked. He whined softly as Erin looked around. The bed was empty and the bathroom door was open.

An uneasy feeling swept over Erin, making her shiver. "Where's Lucy?" she asked Max.

His reply was another whine, this one edged with concern. Erin stepped further inside. Where could the other girl be on such a nasty, cold evening?

Erin spoke reassuringly to Max before she shut him back in the apartment and pounded on Nick's door. There was no answer. Before she sounded a general alarm, Erin needed to make sure that Lucy wasn't somewhere with him, perhaps settling their differences.

Clutching the plate of food that was now too cold to eat, Erin searched the outside area quickly. It was too nasty for basketball, but the kennel area was covered. Hoping to see the other girl at the dog runs with Nick, she rushed around the corner. Her heart sank with disappointment when she saw him leaning against the fence alone.

"What's the matter?" he asked, straightening from where he'd been bending over Lulu, the new addition.

"It's Lucy," Erin admitted, biting her lip. "I can't find her."

"She's in her apartment," he said. "Probably still sulking."

When Erin shook her head and told him she had just been there, his face tensed with alarm.

"I'm getting worried," Erin confessed. "Max was there alone. I was hoping to find Lucy with you."

Nick grabbed her arm. "We'd better round up some help and organize a search party," he said. "Lucy may be in trouble and she shouldn't be out in this cold rain."

"Wait a minute," Erin told him. "If she's outside somewhere,

Max will be able to find her faster than the rest of us put together. Let's get him."

Quickly, she and Nick rushed back to Lucy's unit, while Erin uttered a silent prayer. Spotting Lucy's flashlight, she grabbed it while Nick ducked in next door to get his own. Erin didn't want to think about the living hell Nick would put himself through if anything at all had happened to his little sister.

They ran into Darren when they came out of Lucy's. Erin explained the problem quickly.

"I'll check the office and the other buildings," he said. "Just in case."

Erin was grateful for his calmness. "Thanks," she told him. "Try not to alarm the others."

They needed to find Lucy quickly. It was getting colder by the minute and there was no telling how long she had been gone. Erin fingered her own parka. It was already getting wet.

As soon as she told Max to "find Lucy," he rushed off, down one of the paved trails that snaked into the woods. Erin and Nick rushed after him, but he came running back in a matter of moments. Then Erin pointed and he trotted down a second trail.

"Do you think Lucy might have gone into the woods alone?" she asked Nick. The weather hadn't been so bad earlier. On a nice day, the trails provided an opportunity to enjoy nature; on a dark night like this one, they appeared gloomy and threatening.

"It's hard to know what she'd do when she was upset," Nick admitted, raking a hand through his wet hair. He and Erin were both getting chilled by the stinging rain. Even Max's coat was damp.

They were following the dog down a third trail, flashlights shining in front of them, when they heard him bark.

Darren, who had caught up to them, said, "It sounds like he may have found something."

Immediately, Nick broke into a run. Erin and Darren were right behind him when he rounded the last curve in the trail.

"Oh, my God!" Erin exclaimed when she saw Nick go down on his knees in the mud by a crumpled body lying alongside the paved trail. Nearby, a wheelchair, tipped onto its side, gleamed in the beam from her flashlight.

"It's Lucy!" Nick choked out, reaching to brush the wet, matted hair away from her pale face. The pain in his voice was like a knife through Erin's heart.

Ten

"Is she conscious?" Erin asked, as she rushed over to where Nick knelt in the mud by Lucy's crumpled body. Max kept licking her deathly pale face and whining anxiously.

"Okay, Max. Okay," Nick said, shoving the dog gently aside. For a moment, fear threatened to choke him. Then Max's sharp bark galvanized him into action.

"Lucy?" he demanded, taking one of her hands and chaffing her icy fingers. "Can you hear me?"

Relief flooded through him when his sister's eyes fluttered open in the light from Erin's flashlight. Lucy groaned and moved her head. Nick had to swallow hard as a flood of emotion threatened to swamp his control. He was barely aware of the icy rain stinging his cheeks as Lucy tried to sit up.

"What took you so long?" she asked. She was only wearing a sweater over her blouse and long pants, and she was soaked from the cold rain. Nick sat back on his heels, stripped off his own fleece-lined jacket and wrapped it around her. It was damp but better than nothing.

Max pushed forward to lick Lucy's cheek again and she raised a hand to pat his head.

"Max was the one to find you," Erin said as she ran her hands over Lucy's body, checking for injuries. Behind her, Darren righted the wheelchair.

"This seems to be okay," he said.

"One wheel slipped off the path when I turned around," Lucy said. "I crashed and burned." Her voice faded in and out; her teeth were chattering.

"She feels okay," Erin said quietly. "Lucy, do you hurt any-where?"

"I'm just cold," she moaned.

"You can tell us all about it later," Nick said, scooping her into his arms and rising. "Right now we need to get you to a doctor."

"I don't need a doctor," Lucy argued between shivers. "I need to get Max inside before he gets sick again."

"Don't worry about Max," Darren told her. "I'll look after him while Erin and Nick run you over to Valley General."

"I'm fine," Lucy insisted. "I'm just a little cold is all." Another shiver went through her and Nick gathered her close. "You're freezing."

"I'll bring her chair," Darren said. "Go on. Get her out of the rain."

"Let's take her home first," Erin suggested. "I'll help her into dry clothes and then we'll take her to the emergency room."

"I don't need to go to the hospital," Lucy grumbled again. Her words were punctuated by an explosive sneeze.

"Humor your brother," Erin said briskly, her bossy tone making Nick smile. Now that he knew Lucy was safe, he could breathe again.

"Might as well listen to her," he said with a grin that was only slightly forced. "She won't let up until you do what she says."

Erin's eyes flashed but she didn't deny his words. "Come on," she said instead.

Erin looked up when Nick came out of the examining room where the nurse had taken Lucy.

"The doctor's checking her over now," he said, as he raked a hand through his damp, tousled hair. "He kicked me out."

"Of course he did." Erin wanted to smooth down his hair and comfort him, but wasn't sure how. He had been like a coiled spring as they rushed Lucy back to her apartment and then to the hospital emergency room.

Once here, she had been whisked away while Nick filled out paperwork. As soon as he was done, he left Erin thumbing through a dog-eared magazine and tracked Lucy down.

After a few minutes, during which Nick prowled the waiting area like an angry tiger, the nurse summoned him back to the examination room to see the doctor. Erin followed, determined to hear firsthand how Lucy was doing.

"I need to check on my dog." Erin heard Lucy say as she followed Nick into the room, bisected by a flowered curtain. On one side of the curtain, Lucy was sitting in her wheelchair. Her cheeks were flushed and she wore a mutinous expression. Nick immediately knelt down and took her hand.

"You gave us a scare, peanut."

"This is my brother, and my friend, Erin," she said.

The doctor introduced himself. "She seems to be merely suffering from slight exposure, but we'd like to keep her overnight," he told Nick. "Just to be sure."

"That's fine," Nick replied at the same time that Lucy said, "no way."

"I need to check on Max," she insisted. "He won't sleep if I'm not there."

"Who's Max?" the doctor asked Lucy. "Your little boy?"

"Max can stay with me tonight," Nick said. "Max is her service dog," he explained. "He wasn't with Lucy when she fell because he's had a slight temperature. He's the one who found her, and he got pretty wet when we were out searching."

"Let your brother worry about Max tonight," the doctor said. "If it hadn't been for the dog, you might be a whole lot worse off than you are."

"We'll come back and get you first thing in the morning, okay?" Erin promised, hoping to further ease Lucy's mind.

"See? All taken care of," the doctor said, spreading his hands.

Lucy's expression remained stubborn.

"Let us talk to her," Nick said.

The doctor grinned. "Okay, but don't use any rubber hoses," he said. "I'll be back in a few minutes."

As soon as he had left the room, Nick sat on the edge of the examining table and took Lucy's hand in his.

"You're still cold," he said.

Lucy rolled her eyes and looked across at Erin. "Can't you break me out of here?"

Erin shook her head. "Tomorrow," she said.

"I want to go back to the center." Lucy's tone was fretful.

"Listen," Nick said gently as Erin looked on. "Remember the game we used to play?"

"Which one?"

He sighed. "Whenever you were sick, I would always tell you I'd grant a wish if you'd work hard on getting better."

A smile played at the corners of Lucy's mouth. "Oh, that game."

"Yeah," he said, winking at Erin. Then his expression sobered and he returned his attention to his sister.

"So, what's your wish, little sister?"

Lucy didn't answer for a moment. Instead, her eyes filled with tears and she turned her head away.

"Hey," Nick said softly, catching her chin in his fingers, "don't cry. It'll be okay."

The tender concern in his voice almost brought tears to Erin's eyes, too. She knew how very much he loved his sister, and how much he blamed himself for her condition. Would he ever be able to lay down the burden of guilt he carried?

"So," he was saying as he bent over Lucy in her chair. "What do you want? What's your wish, baby?"

She reached up and gripped both his hands in hers. Her eyes were wide and her lips trembled. "I want my life back," she whispered.

Erin's tears spilled over at her words, and she thought she glimpsed a film of moisture in Nick's eyes, too, but couldn't be sure.

"I want that for you, too," he said, voice husky.

Lucy swallowed as Erin wiped at her cheeks. "I want it back from you, Nick," she continued. "Loosen your grip on me, bro."

Erin saw a lone tear trickle down his tanned cheek before Lucy reached up and wiped it away.

"I don't know what to say," he confessed. "You're my baby sister, and I'm so used to looking out for you." His smile was edged with sadness. "But I will take care of Max until you get out of here, okay? I owe him. We wouldn't have found you so quickly without him."

"If Max had been with me when I fell, he would have gone for help," Lucy said. "And I wouldn't have been out there so long."

"I know that," Nick agreed. "I'll keep him with me tonight, okay?"

"Oh, all right." Lucy might be giving in, but Erin could tell that she wasn't happy about it. "And think about the other stuff."

"I will." He patted her hand as a nurse appeared in the doorway.

"We're ready to move you to a regular room," she said.

"Don't wait for me," Lucy told Nick and Erin. "Go home and take care of Max."

Nick bent over to give her a kiss on the cheek, and then Erin squeezed her hand. "We'll see you in the morning," she promised. "Get some rest." She left the room so Nick would have a few moments with his sister.

When he came out, his eyes were suspiciously red, but Erin pretended not to notice. Nick stretched an arm across her shoulders. "Let's go take care of Max," he said.

Nick felt like a ball of tension when he finally went to bed that night. Max lay on the floor next to him, and Nick patted the dog's thick fur before he turned over and wadded the pillow under his head. He knew it was going to be a long, sleepless night.

As soon as she had reassured herself that Max was no worse for the chill he had gotten earlier, Erin had given Nick a considering look and asked if he was all right. When he had answered in the affirmative, she left to tell the others about Lucy and to finish some chores. Nick hadn't laid eyes on her since.

Maybe that contributed to his wakefulness.

He shifted again on the bed, flipped onto his back and stacked his hands beneath his head. Staring into the darkness, listening to Max's even breathing, he acknowledged just how important the dog had become to his sister. He pictured the two of them working on a class exercise, dealing with the public on a field trip, sharing a look of complete understanding that Nick couldn't hope to comprehend.

What if Lucy was right—that he couldn't have prevented the accident—and that he *didn't* owe her? What if all Nick's good intentions, to take care of her, to keep her safe and to make things easier for her, were just a sop to his conscience? Or worse yet, an excuse to avoid dealing with the real issues between himself and Erin? Issues like feelings and trust and commitment. Had he been using his obligation to Lucy as a reason to hide from life and its uncertainties? From the possibility of rejection?

Was he using guilt as a shield? Denial as a safety net?

While the questions continued to torment him, there was a soft knock at the door.

Max uttered a warning growl. Nick's heartbeat kicked into a higher gear as he rolled off the bed and pulled on the jeans he had left on the floor.

"Okay, boy," Nick told Max, who had gotten to his feet. "You stay here." He took a deep breath and crossed the room in his bare feet. When he opened the door, Erin stood in a pool of light wearing a lime green slicker over the same clothes she'd had on earlier. She looked tired. There were faint smudges beneath her eyes. Around her, the sound of the steady rain filled the night. Her hair was damp and curls sprang up all over her head. She was beautiful.

"Did I wake you?" she asked, eyeing Nick's bare chest and unsnapped jeans. "I know it's late and I wondered if you were able to sleep."

He stepped away from the door. "As a matter of fact, I wasn't," he told her as warmth drizzled through him like honey. "Come on in." He switched on a small table lamp. "I may start believing in Santa Claus and the Tooth Fairy again."

Clearly, Erin could make no sense of what he was saying. "Why?"

He grinned. "I was wishing you were here."

She looked pleased but tried to hide it. "They're as real as the pillow tag police," she said seriously.

It was Nick's turn to be confused. "Excuse me?" he said. "Pillow tag police?"

Her grin widened and she shook her damp hair and wrinkled her nose. "You know those tags on pillows?" she asked, slipping out of the wet slicker. "The ones that say it's illegal to remove them?"

Nick began to chuckle as he tossed the slicker over the back of a chair. "Don't tell me. The pillow tag police go around and—"

She nodded. "Of course. I thought everyone knew that."

"You made it all up."

"No, I didn't," she insisted. "Let me see your pillow and I'll show you the tag."

He shook his head, realizing she had already dispelled some of the tension he had been unable to suppress. "I'll take your word for it."

"I should think so." Erin glanced at the unmade bed. "I got you up," she said.

If you only knew, Nick thought wryly. "No," he said. "You didn't. I was tossing and turning anyway. Keeping Max awake, I'm afraid." Suddenly, he felt awkward. All he wanted was to grab her and bury his nose in her hair, to bury himself in her warmth and to feel *alive*. His hands shook and he shoved them into the back pockets of his jeans.

"Uh, do you want a cup of coffee?" he asked. "I could make some." He glanced at the kitchen counter, lowered for handicapped access. He was pretty sure there was still some instant in the single cupboard.

"No, thanks." In the faint light, Erin looked as nervous as he felt.

Then a curious sense of rightness filled Nick, calming him, and he moved closer. Lucy wanted her life back. He could have a life, too, if he was willing to reach for it. Maybe it was time to try.

"In that case," he said softly, stopping when he was right in front of Erin, "there's something I'd like."

Her expression was wary. "What's that?"

He lifted his hands slowly and cupped her shoulders, almost afraid he was going to spook her. "You."

She seemed to melt into him as she flowed closer and leaned her cheek against his bare chest. Her arms went around his waist as his slid down her back. Her breath on his skin sent shivers of awareness coursing through him. The blood drained from his brain and settled much lower, leaving him dizzy and aching.

Erin snuggled closer as his arms tightened around her and he groaned softly. Need filled him.

"I had an idea you might be lonesome," she said, sounding pleased.

Immediately, Nick gripped her waist hard and held her away from him. He looked down into her wide eyes. "It's more than that," he muttered, knowing before he spoke again that the words he was about to say were true, had been true almost since he had first met her.

It was time to abandon caution and reach for the gusto. "I love you," he whispered.

Erin's feathery brows rose until they disappeared beneath her bangs. "You don't need to—"

He cut her off. "Yes, I do. I need to tell you how I feel," he said. "Don't you dare believe for a New York minute that all I need is a diversion to get me through the night. Maybe that's a very small part of it, but that's not what this is about and I want you to know it, right up front."

Erin backed away a step. "Are you sure? Because if you aren't—"

His smile came easy, easier than any smile he'd had in the last couple of years.

"I may be kinda slow," he drawled, moving closer to her again, "but I'm not dumb. I've been trying to fool myself since the first time you told me to lighten up. But I saw tonight how important Max is to Lucy—"

At the sound of his name, Max rose from where he'd been lying down and came over, wagging his tale. He shoved his muzzle into Nick's hand.

"Good boy," Nick told him. "Now go back to sleep." To his surprise, Max padded back to his chosen spot by the bed, turned around twice and collapsed in a furry heap.

"Where was I?" Nick muttered.

"Telling me you love me because you've figured out how important Max is to Lucy," Erin recited, looking confused.

"Well, the two things probably aren't connected as closely as all that," Nick told her as he moved closer to the bed, his arm around her waist. "As I was saying—"

"I thought you didn't remember," Erin interrupted.

"Shhh. As I was saying, I may be slow, but eventually I figure out what's going on. Lucy wants me to give her a chance. Perhaps it's time to give *me* a chance, too."

"That sounds logical," Erin whispered. "Tell me again."

"About how important Max is to Lucy?" he teased her, keeping his expression solemn.

"No!" Erin slapped at his arm. "About what you said about me," she coaxed. "Tell me again."

"You mean the part about how I feel toward you?" Nick pretended to guess.

She nodded, eyes misty. "Yeah. That part." For an instant, she looked so vulnerable that it almost broke his heart, and then the look was gone.

"I love you," he said, feeling protective. As soon as the words were out, he bent his head and kissed her. His voice deepened. "Love you," he repeated on a rough growl of need.

"I love you, too," she echoed, and his heart thundered with relief.

He couldn't keep from bowing his head to nibble at the sensitive, perfumed length of her neck, couldn't keep his senses from swimming as her scent filled his head. He burrowed one hand beneath the waistband of her sweatshirt and caressed the smooth expanse of her back.

"Mmm, soft," he murmured against her ear as heat and need and joy filled him.

Erin slipped her hands across his bare shoulders, her touch as light as the flutter of a hummingbird's wings. He ran his fingers up her spine, savoring the graceful curve. She shivered. As she lifted her arms from around his neck, he pulled the sweatshirt over her head. Her hair was standing on end.

The smoldering hunger in her gaze that she made no effort to hide reminded him of a closeup he had seen once of a lioness in a nature movie. The big cat had been stalking her prey. If Erin was stalking him, he was ready to surrender.

He dropped the damp sweatshirt to the chair with her forgotten slicker and reached for the snap of her jeans. She stood before him so trustingly that he felt humbled. He leaned forward and kissed the pearly skin above the curve of her bra. Her gasp of pleasure caressed his ear. Echoed throughout his being.

Slowly, he drew the zip of her jeans downward. As he did, nibbling his way across her collarbone, she slipped her fingers into the open waistband of the pants he had pulled on when he had first heard the knock on his door.

"Oh," she murmured as she discovered that he wore nothing beneath the denim. His arousal strained against the snaps of his fly, increasing his ache. His stomach muscles danced with reaction as her fingers skated lower. They sifted through the course hair until she brushed against his most sensitive flesh. He thought his knees would buckle.

"Ah, wait a minute," he gritted through clenched teeth. Her touch felt so good he wanted to thrust himself closer yet. "Maybe that's not such a good idea."

Erin's eyes were wide when she leaned back and looked into his. The little minx knew exactly what she was doing to him!

"Why not?" she asked, batting her lashes.

"Trust me," he muttered, starting to ease her jeans over her slim hips. His own fingers skimmed down across the wisp of satin covering her feminine secrets. He felt her shiver of reaction. Going onto his knees before her, he held onto her jeans while she stepped out of them. Her hand gripped his shoulder for balance. He tossed the jeans over the back of the couch. Then he leaned forward and planted an open-mouthed kiss on her mound beneath the sheer fabric of her panties.

Erin's fingers tightened on his shoulder until he could feel her nails pressing into his flesh. "Oh, my," she gasped.

Getting to his feet, he nibbled his way back up her stomach to the sheer lace of her bra. With his hands flat against her back, he sucked hard on first one nipple and then the other through the thin fabric. Then he freed the clasp and slipped off the scrap of lingerie. Holding her, he arched her gently over his arm and explored the bare, ripe curves of her breasts while she moaned her pleasure. Her nipples were hard buttons begging for attention.

Nick resisted. He backed Erin to the bed and gently laid her down. Then he pushed off his own jeans and followed her.

The feel of her body beneath his made Nick forget all about the idea he had entertained—of drawing out the loving until they were both mad with desire. Instead, he slipped one hard thigh between her legs, pressing it intimately against her veiled heat and sliding it gently up and down. She arched off the bed and her hands, which had been on his back, slid to his buttocks.

Nick rolled away from her, opened the drawer and took out a foil packet. He ripped it open and dealt with the contents. Then he went back to Erin, who looked, in the glow from the small lamp, as if she had been created just for him from pure gold. His hands skimmed the length of her, stealing away the last scrap of her clothing.

When he bent to gather her close, she met him halfway, tangling her legs with his. He slipped his hand down between their bodies, seeking the center of her desire. As soon as he found the plump, delicate petals, he eased his finger between them and stroked her. She cried out and pressed closer.

Easing her to her side, Nick faced her and pulled her legs up, around his waist. Then he urged her closer still, and entered her silken heat.

Erin's hands on his buttocks tightened, pulling him deep, as her thighs gripped him harder. Caught in passion's grip, he increased the speed and power of his thrusts and hurled them both closer to the very edge of sanity. Then, holding her tight, he took them over.

The last thing Nick heard before his own hoarse cry of pleasure was Erin's moan of fulfillment.

Erin woke before Nick did and lay watching him sleep. His mouth was relaxed. His face for once was free from strain.

She recalled his words of love and wondered if he was any closer to letting Lucy go. Erin wished she could help, could somehow ease the pain for him, but knew it was something he would have to do himself. And prayed he could find the strength for it.

As for her, it was enough to lie quietly and watch him. His thick lashes lay against his burnished skin like cutouts of black felt and the beginnings of dark whiskers shadowed his lean cheeks. He looked like a pirate who had just taken a moment to rest his eyes.

Max rose and stretched. Then he came over and sniffed at Erin's bare arm above the bedspread. His whiskers tickled and she tried to slip from beneath the covers without waking Nick, but he turned over and his eyes fluttered open.

"I'm just letting Max out," she murmured, bending to kiss his forehead. "Go back to sleep."

As she padded naked over to the door and opened it, standing well hidden behind the solid panel, she glanced back at Nick. He had raised his head to watch her. His hair stuck out at odd angles and he was grinning. As soon as Max was outside, she shut the door.

"Good morning," Nick said in a deep, sleep-roughened voice.

"Good morning, yourself. I didn't mean to wake you. I thought I'd slip away as soon as Max came back."

"Better dress first," Nick drawled.

She made a face as Max scratched on the door. Letting him back in, she rubbed his ears and told him what a good boy he was.

"Come here," Nick commanded softly.

Erin looked up, to see which of them he was addressing, her or the dog. Nick's intense gaze left no question as to whom he had summoned.

Erin crossed to the bed, slightly embarrassed at the thoroughness with which he was studying her bare body. She should have put on his shirt instead of parading around in the altogether.

"What time is it, anyway?" Nick muttered. They both glanced at the bedside clock.

"It's too late," Erin groaned, her senses awakened by his blatant perusal. "I've got to get out of here."

"We have to pick Lucy up in a couple of hours," Nick said.

"Yes," she agreed, making a concerted effort to collect her scattered wits and tamp down the fires of passion he had aroused so effortlessly. "And first I have to shower and change and put in an appearance at breakfast."

"Me, too," he agreed with a smile that was downright roguish. "Let's shower together. You know how big the stall is." He referred to the oversized shower that could accommodate a wheelchair. Or two healthy adults, standing close together. "Think of the water we'd save." His smile was hopeful, but Erin only grinned and shook her head.

"Nice try."

Nick frowned as he slid from beneath the covers. She stared at his nude body and swallowed, mouth suddenly dry. Everything they had shared the night before, as well as the words of love they had exchanged, came rushing back.

"Well," she said, clearing her throat and calculating quickly. "I guess that no one has any business being out and about for at least another half hour, anyway."

As soon as the van had cleared the gates at the end of the center's driveway, Nick surprised Erin by pulling over to the shoulder of the county road and cutting the engine.

"What are you doing?" she demanded, thinking there was something wrong with the van. "Lucy's expecting us."

"Lucy can wait for the few minutes this will take," Nick said, smiling mysteriously. He cradled her face in his hands and dropped a tender kiss on her mouth. Warmth exploded inside her at the familiar taste and feel of him. Her hands, resting on his forearms, tightened possessively as she kissed him back. Nick's breath caught in his throat. His lips turned greedy. Finally, when Erin was dizzy with want and Nick's own response was clearly at flash point, he let her go. Then he stared deep into her eyes until she squirmed with discomfort.

"What is it?"

He surprised her by taking her hand and pressing it over his heart. "I think I'm on overload," he groaned. "How am I ever going to give you up?"

Erin had been trying hard not to think about his departure for Eugene, which was drawing closer each day. After he had told her that he loved her, she wondered if he expected to conduct a long-distance romance or if his feelings would fade with the miles.

Now his light tone confused her. "I don't know," she said, not sure what kind of response he was looking for. "How *are* you going to be able to give me up?" The thought of his leaving was a painful one and had no simple solution. "I guess we knew going in how this would end," she said lamely, not expecting him to answer.

"But it doesn't have to be that way," he mused, watching her intently.

"It doesn't?" she echoed. Her heart began to pound. "What are you getting at?"

"You could come to Eugene with me."

His words stunned her. She had no idea he had been thinking along those lines. In some ways, they still didn't know each other all that well. Her heart leaped at the idea.

Then reality raised its ugly head. "How could I do that?" she asked. "The service center, everything I've worked so hard to build, it's all here in Monroe." Did he expect her to leave everything behind and follow him home? Like a stray animal with no place to go?

He was moving too fast for her. She couldn't think clearly while he was watching her so intently.

At her reference to the center, his gaze finally faltered. He studied the leaden sky beyond the van's windshield as if it was the most fascinating sight he had ever seen.

"You could find something else to do," he said. "You could even go back to school, become a veterinarian if you wanted."

"How did you know about that?" she demanded.

He looked at her and shrugged. "I think it was Anna who mentioned it."

Pain sliced through Erin. Had he so little respect for what she did that he could casually suggest she find something else to fill her time? As if she was a child who needed to be entertained when he was busy.

"Or you could stay home," he continued. "We could start a family. Don't you want children?"

Was he talking about marriage? She wasn't sure. The thought of bearing Nick's children took her breath away. And his power over her raised her hackles. "Of course I want children. Eventually."

After a moment that ached with silence, she asked, "Does that mean that you'd find someone else to run Blackwood Construction and stay home, too?"

A wary expression came over Nick's face. "What do you mean?"

She straightened away from him. "Wouldn't that be even better than having one parent at home?" she asked, "Having two there?"

His cheeks darkened and his eyes began to glitter. "Maybe suggesting that you stay home was a bad idea," he admitted. "But there's a lot you could find to do in Eugene. The important thing is that we would be together. At least that's what's important to me."

"Then why don't you stay up here?" she asked. "We could be together here just as well as in Oregon."

"I have a business to run," he exclaimed.

"Bingo. So do I."

There was another moment of silence while he appeared to consider what she had said. If only he would come up with a workable solution! He frowned and she turned away, blinking back tears. How could he profess to love her when he didn't really understand anything about her?

"I think you're looking for someone to take Lucy's place," she blurted.

His eyes narrowed. "What do you mean by that?"

"You want someone whose life you can control."

Nick reared back as if she had slapped him. Erin knew she had gone too far, but she couldn't take back what she had said. It was the truth.

Nick turned the key in the ignition. Sadly, Erin listened to the engine catch. She wished they could go back—erase everything after he had kissed her and start again.

"I guess I wasn't being very realistic," he said. His voice was steady, emotionless. As if their discussion hadn't really affected him. As if he had already cut his losses.

"I don't see any way out," Erin said in a small voice. "You have your work, your life, and I have mine."

If Nick heard the regret in her voice, he ignored it as he signalled and pulled back onto the road. "I wasn't looking for someone to take Lucy's place," he said, almost as an afterthought. "Lucy will be returning to Eugene with me. That's her home."

Erin put one hand on the door handle. "Would you mind going to the hospital alone?" she asked, pride keeping her voice steady. "I think I'd like to walk back to the center. I want to be by myself for a while, and you'd probably like some time with your sister, anyway."

Nick hesitated. "If that's what you want," he said finally, signalling and once again pulling onto the shoulder as another car passed them. "Are you okay?"

"I'm fine."

"Well, I won't be too long." He searched her face as if looking for clues. His own expression was blank and Erin wondered if he felt any real pain from her rejection. His invitation had been so casual she hadn't really considered the feelings behind it. She had been too involved with her own keen sense of disappointment. How could everything go so wrong so quickly?

"Make my excuses to Lucy, will you?" she asked, opening the door.

"Sure. Are you positive you're all right?"

Erin climbed out and glanced back at him. "I'll be fine." She was pretty sure that was she was saying was a lie, but she had no intentions of letting Nick see her pain.

"Okay." He looked relieved.

As soon as he drove away, she knew she wasn't going to be fine. Very soon he would be driving away for real, for the last time.

How would she ever survive it?

Eleven

During the time that was left before graduation, Erin threw herself into her work. She didn't know what, if anything, Nick might have told Lucy to explain away the brittle politeness between the two of them. If Lucy wondered, she didn't question Erin.

As graduation day grew closer, Jane, Freddie and Lucy bounced between jubilation and despair.

"She doesn't mind me anymore!" Freddie cried after a disastrous workout with Queenie. "She's forgotten everything."

"Be patient," Erin coaxed. "Repeat the commands slowly and give her time to obey. She can tell if you're upset, you know."

Freddie nodded anxiously and led his border collie off for more practice.

"I know I'm going to blank out at the written exam!" Lucy exclaimed. "Tests make my brain overheat. Can't I take this one orally?"

"You'll do fine," Erin said, trying to reassure her. "Have Nick drill you on the commands. You use them all the time and you take a test every morning. Quit worrying!"

"I'll blow the field test," Jane wailed. "I'll get self conscious and Ranger will sense it. He won't listen and I'll go home without a dog."

"You've had plenty of practice," Erin told her. "Just act the same as you did with Dottie."

It seemed to Erin that everyone but Nick approached her about the final exams. He was almost conspicuous by his absence in class, or at least by the distance he kept between himself and Erin.

Normally, the last few days before graduation and the ceremony itself were a favorite time for her, the payoff for all the hard work spent training dogs, soliciting funds and conducting the class to mold human and animal into a working team. Jane, Freddie and Lucy had become as dear to Erin as any of her other students.

Nevertheless, this time, she just wanted boot camp to be over so that the students, their dogs and any relatives who might be hanging around would go home and leave her alone.

Seeing Nick every day, wondering what he was thinking, what—if anything—he was feeling, wore away at her composure like waves undercutting a cliff. She thought about trying to talk to him but, unless she could think of a solution to their dilemma, or unless she was willing to leave the center and go to Eugene with him, there was no point.

In the evenings, darker and colder now as October drew to a close, she spent a lot of time with the younger dogs, especially Lulu. The black Lab was a bit of a clown and her antics often made Erin smile. Still, the renewed enthusiasm she usually felt when she saw another puppy turn into a responsible canine companion was sadly missing this time. She hoped it would reappear once a certain Blackwood male had left for good.

Sometimes when she was trying to sleep in the bed that had suddenly become too wide and too empty, she was tempted to go to Nick and beg him to take her with him. But she wasn't even sure his offer was still open. Maybe he had come to his senses and found he didn't really love her; he had only gotten caught up in a bizarre mixture of good sex and homesickness. Perhaps he considered himself lucky that she had spurned his no doubt impulsive offer. Maybe he no longer wanted a woman who would choose a pack of dogs over him.

Nick spent his evenings in his apartment, working on a set of plans he had been toying with. If Lucy didn't need him to drill her on class material, he holed up there after dinner each evening. He erased and redid the plans until they were exactly right. When he was done, he rolled them up carefully and stood them in a corner.

Then, to keep his mind off Erin, he began idly sketching a building complex unlike anything he had ever done before. He told himself he was only doodling, but when Lucy dropped by, he slid his sketch pad under the newspaper.

All Lucy wanted to talk to him about was living in Seattle. He was surprised at how organized she was in her quest for information from the various agencies that could help her. Apparently Anna had given her a few brochures. Since then, when Lucy wasn't in class or studying, she was burning up her phone company calling card.

"I talked to a woman about getting a bus pass today," she said when Nick saw her at lunch. "They're sending me an application to the community college," she told him at dinner. "I talked to someone about an agency that lists accessible apartments," she said when he answered her knock at his door in the evening. She worked harder than he could remember her working on anything before; manicuring her nails, experimenting with makeup and doing upper body exercises that she said Erin had told her would tone her arms and shoulders.

Far from giving up, burning out or losing enthusiasm, Lucy was expanding her battle plan. Despite his misgivings, he was impressed. And cautiously hopeful that she would succeed.

Everything in his life was spinning beyond his control. Lucy didn't seem to need either his help or his advice, his own heart seemed bent on getting itself broken without his consent, even the business was doing okay without him.

Day after day, Erin taught class with a steady patience and a cheerful smile that showed Nick she wasn't mourning his imminent departure nearly as much as he was. Only pride kept a bland smile of indifference plastered on his face when he wanted to scowl.

Erin saw that smile and wished Nick would find somewhere else to hang out and someone else to torment.

Graduation was held on a Saturday. The morning began with a written test that covered everything the applicants had learned. It was followed by lunch at a nice restaurant on the Everett waterfront that the applicants were too nervous to enjoy and a scavenger hunt at a nearby mall. While Erin observed her students and their dogs, taking notes on her clipboard, they collected items that would be returned to the shops when the hunt was over: a cassette tape by Pearl Jam, a package of off-black panty hose, a candy bar with nuts, a pair of size six women's sandals, a paperback mystery, a man's blue necktie, a red umbrella and a box of goldfish food, to name a few. Each team had ninety minutes to bring back the items on their list.

Meanwhile, Anna was back at the center correcting the written exams. No one was awarded a service dog until Erin was completely convinced they could care for the animal and would derive the full benefits from having it in their life.

While Erin made notes about the field exam, Nick and Darren stood by in case of problems. Erin did her best to ignore Nick's masculine presence in his usual jeans and a worn leather bomber jacket, with a lock of dark hair falling onto his forehead. When three girls walked by and he returned their smiles with a jaunty salute, she was tempted to brain him with her clipboard. Instead, her gaze collided with his and she hurried away to check on Freddie's progress.

Nick had been instructed not to speak to Lucy or the other two students unless absolutely necessary.

"Afraid I'll slip one of them the black panty hose?" he couldn't resist teasing. He'd give a lot to see Erin smile at him instead of at Freddie or Max or even Darren. Instead she had flushed and looked away.

"No. I'm afraid you might distract Lucy and cause her to lose points."

Nick's smile was strained. "Okay, boss, I'll behave."

"Thank you." Her voice was low, making him sorry he had tried to tease her.

Back at the center, he was glad to hear that all three students had passed both tests. How could Erin bear to fail anyone, to send them home empty handed? After seeing how hard they worked, he didn't think he could have.

"Congratulations," she told them. "At graduation this afternoon, each of you will receive a diploma and your dog's registration papers, and you'll get a chance to meet the puppy trainer responsible for their first year of orientation."

Freddie let out a whoop of excitement, Jane blinked rapidly and bowed her head, and Lucy hugged first Max and then Nick. After he had returned Lucy's hug and congratulated her, he saw Erin wiping surreptitiously at her eyes. For the first time, Nick realized the emotional toll this job demanded of her. It gave him something to think about as he watched Lucy, Freddie and Jane hugging each other.

The impromptu celebration in the parking lot was highlighted by the arrival of Freddie's family in a dented station wagon.

"Mom! Dad!" he cried, waving wildly and wheeling himself over to the car. "I passed. I get to take Queenie home." Freddie's dad hugged him and his mom began to cry.

Nick's gaze shifted, colliding with Erin's. For a moment, they exchanged a look free from animosity. Then she gave him a watery smile. He was about to say something, he had no idea what, when Lucy called his name.

"When are Mom and Dad getting here?" she asked impatiently.

He glanced at his watch as he went over to her. "Any time now. I talked to them before they left Eugene this morning. Nothing could keep them away."

When Nick looked back at Erin, she was surrounded by Freddie's family, who were all talking and gesturing at once. He glanced around and caught Darren watching them.

"How are things going?" the other man asked. Nick knew he didn't miss much, and he wondered how much Darren had figured out about him and Erin.

Nick shrugged. "I guess I'm eager to get back to work," he said. "Where *I'm* the boss."

Darren didn't miss Nick's reference to his chores here. "Thanks for all your help," he said, clapping Nick on the back. "If you ever want a job . . ." His voice trailed off and he grinned.

"I'd need more than bed and board, though," Nick kidded.

Darren scratched his chin and pretended to consider. "Minimum wage and you lug the dog food," he offered.

Nick shook his head. "I think I'd better stay in Oregon."

Darren glanced over to where Erin was still talking to Freddie and his family. "Going home alone?" he asked lightly.

Nick followed his gaze. "No," he said grimly. "I'm taking Lucy and Max back with me."

Darren let out a sigh. "Maybe we'll see you again."

Nick shrugged. "Maybe."

Erin kept sneaking looks at Nick and Darren, wondering what they were talking about. Anna had already quizzed her about Nick and his departure, and Erin wasn't sure how much she would have told Darren about Erin's admission that he had asked her to go and she had refused. Not that Darren would repeat any confidences to Nick. Still, their serious expressions made her nervous.

The graduation ceremony was a real celebration, with puppy trainers, volunteers, former alumni of the center and financial sponsors present as well as interested and supportive townspeople from Monroe. The event was held at the community hall in town, since the turnout had grown bigger than any room at the center could hold.

Erin stood at the back of the hall, wearing a royal blue dress and navy high heeled sandals, and watched people file in and find seats. The organist from a local church played soft piano music. Caroline Burns, the woman who usually worked with the dogs, had come in earlier and helped get the hall ready. Now she turned around in her seat and waved. Erin smiled and waved back.

Her three graduates would sit in the front. It had been a hectic month and she knew they were glad it was almost over.

"Hello again, Miss McKenzie."

Erin turned to greet Burt and Muriel Blackwood, Nick and Lucy's parents. She had met them earlier when they arrived from Eugene.

"Your training facility is very impressive," Burt said. "Lucy took us on a tour."

His wife, Muriel, murmured her agreement. Burt Blackwood was a forceful man with silver hair and Muriel seemed to be a sweet, rather shy woman. Nick and Lucy both had her eyes.

"Thank you," Erin told them. "I've had a lot of help. Lucy, here, has been one of my best students." She bent down to give her a hug. "Enjoy this," she said. "You certainly earned it."

"I feel incomplete without Max," Lucy complained. The dogs would be handed over formally during graduation.

Behind her chair, Nick stood watching Erin. He gave her a crooked smile but said nothing as he filed passed. It took her several minutes after he had gone to his seat to subdue the tension that gripped her. She greeted more people and finally glanced at her watch. The graduates were here and it was almost time to start.

She took a deep breath and walked down a side aisle to the podium up front.

"Thank you all for coming," she said into the microphone. "This is a big day for our graduates and for all of us at Northwest Service Dogs." She went on to explain a little bit about the center. A former graduate who had just signed a recording contract in Nashville sang an inspirational song about love and support and then an attorney from Seattle spoke briefly about the ways his dog had changed his life.

"I thought the car accident I was in six years ago had ended my career," he told the audience. He patted the chocolate Lab at his side and the dog barked, soliciting chuckles from the crowd. "Then Marty showed me that life just keeps getting better."

There was a burst of applause and Erin returned to the podium.

"Now comes the part we've all been waiting for," she said. While the pianist played "Pomp and Circumstance" softly, she introduced the graduates, one by one. When Freddie came up, he was wearing a white shirt and a bright red bow tie. His eyes were sparkling behind his thick glasses and his cheeks were flushed.

Erin presented him with his certificate and shook his hand.

"Thanks!" he shouted. "Where's my dog?"

Erin pointed down the center aisle. Then she introduced the puppy trainer who had raised Queenie and been responsible for her first year of schooling. Everyone applauded as the trainer, a teenage girl from Tacoma, escorted the border collie to the front and presented her to Freddie. They hugged, he thanked her while Erin watched tearfully, and then he turned to the crowd.

"I got my dog!" he announced. Everyone laughed and applauded while he went back to the front row, Queenie trotting proudly at his side with his certificate in her mouth.

Next, Erin introduced Jane. Ranger's puppy trainer was a retired Marine from Camano Island. He had been sitting with Erin's parents, who attended as many graduations as they could. Jane was beaming and several of her friends applauded loudly as she was presented with her certificate and dog.

When it was Lucy's turn to come up, she was crying openly. She gave Erin another exuberant hug.

"Thank you for making this possible," she said quietly while Erin blinked back her own tears.

"You're very special," she told the younger girl with one hand over the mike. "I expect you to come back and speak at future graduations when you've become a successful model."

"I will," Lucy promised fervently. "Now I want my dog."

Erin laughed and introduced the trainer, who brought Max forward. As soon as the exchange was made and Lucy had returned to the front row, the audience rose and gave the three graduates a standing ovation.

"Thanks for coming," Erin told everyone. "Please join us for punch and cookies served in the back of the room by our wonderful volunteers." She had barely finished speaking when Nick stood and raised his hand.

"Miss McKenzie, may I say something before we break up?" he asked. He was holding a long roll of paper.

Erin couldn't imagine what he intended. Surely he wouldn't air his negative views now? His confident, relaxed expression revealed nothing.

"Of course," she said. What other choice did she have? Hoping she was right, Erin introduced Nick and stepped back from the podium.

"I won't keep you from the refreshments for long," he promised the crowd with a smile. "I just want to announce that my company, Blackwood Construction, is donating a new exercise wing and spa to the center, as a small thank you to Erin and her staff. Construction will start as soon as she and I can work out the details and obtain the necessary permits."

Erin was stunned by his announcement. She had described to him the addition she pictured, with space for exercise equipment and a specially built hot tub, but it was something she wouldn't be able to afford for years, if ever.

There was a brief silence, followed by a burst of applause as Nick unrolled the paper he held. "These are the plans I've drawn up," he told her. "Why don't you look them over and perhaps we can discuss them before we leave, if you have time."

Erin searched his face, hardly able to speak as she took the plans from him. What did this mean? As a gesture of gratitude, it was unbelievably generous. As a peace offering, it was the best thing he could have given her. Short of himself.

"Thank you," she said softly. After more clapping, the crowd began to drift toward the refreshments at the back of the room.

Before either Nick or Erin could say anything else, Lucy and his parents came forward. Amid the general conversation that ensued, Erin kept sneaking looks at the plans and then at Nick. If nothing else, she would see him again when his crew came up to build the addition. That was the best part.

Nick would have liked to take longer to discuss the exercise wing with Erin, but she was kept busy thanking everyone for coming. They all wanted to speak to her, and Nick could understand why. She had a warm smile and a few words for everyone. Plus she knew most of their names.

Accepting defeat, Nick stepped aside. The few minutes he had taken to explain the plans to her, and her assurance that the wing was exactly as she had pictured it, would have to be enough for him.

Lucy and the rest of his family were the last ones to say goodbye. They had a long drive back to Eugene and Nick knew his parents were eager to leave.

Lucy had mentioned that she was calling Nita Blue from the modeling agency on Monday, but that was all she had said.

"Thanks for everything," she told Erin, Anna and Darren as Nick loaded their bags into his car. He came forward to lift her onto the front seat, but she stopped him.

While he watched, she positioned her chair and levered herself over without any assistance.

"I've been practicing," she said proudly when she was settled. Nick loaded her wheelchair into the trunk, putting off the moment he had to face Erin. Max sat in solitary splendor on the back seat, his head stuck out the open window.

After a last good-bye, their parents got in the other car and left. Nick shut Lucy's door and turned to Erin, wishing for a moment of privacy. He glanced at Anna and Darren, who were watching him with undisguised interest. Darren winked.

Nick could see the shadows in Erin's blue eyes. Maybe this was as hard for her as it was for him. The thought cheered him. He'd be back to build the addition. They would talk again then.

Looking at Erin, so pretty in the blue dress, he knew he couldn't leave without touching her. He didn't care who was watching. Her eyes widened when he stepped closer and she realized his intentions.

"Nick," she squeaked as he pulled her into his arms.

"This is to remember me by," he muttered for her ears alone. He held her tight and bent his head. The kiss, which he deliberately kept short, wasn't nearly enough. The flash of her response burned through him and then he let her go. Before he could give in to temptation and kiss her again, he circled his car and opened the driver door. Only then did he glance back.

Erin's expression revealed nothing of what she might be feeling. Her cheeks, however, were bright pink and her mouth trembled. Memorizing her face, he got into the car.

As they drove down the road, Lucy, as if sensing his jumbled emotions, didn't say a word.

Erin barely noticed when Darren and Anna went inside, leaving her alone. Right until Nick got in the car, she had hoped he might say something, anything, about seeing her again. He hadn't, though, and that last kiss had only served to confuse her more than she already was. Had he meant it as a good-bye or a token of his continuing interest?

Well, if he thought she was going to wait around for him to make a move, he was mistaken, she thought angrily. She had work to do, and a life to live. And no time to dwell on Nick Blackwood and wonder about his motives. It was over and she had to accept that.

Refusing to look up for a last glimpse of the black Mercedes, Erin went back to the office to study the plans he had left behind.

"Well," Lucy said, breaking the silence as she looked out the window of Nick's car, "I can't wait to call Nita on Monday. Then I'll have to go back up to Seattle and find an apartment near the bus line."

Out of the corner of his eye, Nick saw her turn to watch for his reaction. A week ago he would have brought up all the reasons why her idea was foolhardy in the extreme. Now he remained silent. Lucy had passed the course and gotten her dog. She deserved the chance to prove she could run her own life.

Seeing her lying in the rain with Max standing over her, licking her pale face, had finally made Nick realize she was going to make her own mistakes, with or without his approval. He loved her too much to stand in her way any longer.

"How are you getting to Seattle?" he asked as he passed an r.v. that was meandering down the center lane.

Lucy sighed. "I'll take the bus." He watched her nibble at her lip. "Would you give me a ride to the station?"

Nick had a vision of her trying to cope with her luggage and with Max. "Play your cards right and I'll take you all the way to Seattle," he said. "If I can get off work. Dad doesn't seem to be in any hurry to hand back the reins of command."

"Oh, I don't know," Lucy disagreed. "He and Mom were talking about some trip to Costa Rica with another retired couple. He'll probably be happy to leave the business and the winter weather behind."

Nick snorted. Keeping the various projects on schedule through torrents of rain, unexpected snowstorms and sudden drops in temperature was always a challenge. He found himself looking forward to it. He needed a challenge he could win.

Erin sat looking out the living room window of her parents' house watching the rain. It was Thanksgiving and the center was closed for the long weekend. Everyone on the staff had gone to spend the holiday with relatives and Caroline had promised to take care of the dogs.

For once, Erin didn't miss being at the center like she usually did. Since the last class had graduated at the end of October, she had been following her busy schedule more or less on automatic pilot.

Watching the clouds move across the gloomy sky, she recalled the last phone call she had taken from Lucy earlier that week.

The agency had decided to start using handicapped models out of their Portland office. Lucy had found an apartment, moved in and enrolled at the local community college. She would be taking computer courses and had already completed her first modeling assignment for a chain of discount hardware stores.

She mentioned that Nick and her parents visited often. Erin wanted to hear more about Nick, but was too stubborn to ask.

"He's been busy," Lucy said, as if she heard her unspoken question. "He looks tired and I'm worried about him. He doesn't smile much."

"Maybe he has problems at work," Erin suggested.

Lucy made a rude sound of disbelief and then changed the subject. After a few more moments, they promised to keep in touch and hung up.

Rising from the sofa where she had been curled up since her mother had kicked her out of the kitchen, Erin decided to see if it was time to set the table. Her aunt was basting the turkey, her two cousins were playing outside despite the rain and her father, uncle and grandfather were watching a football game on TV. Erin pasted on a smile and headed into the kitchen.

"She just hasn't been herself," she heard her mother say. "I think it has something to do with a young man from Oregon that she met, but Erin isn't talking."

Before Aunt Ida could offer an opinion on Erin's love life, she coughed discreetly and pushed open the swinging door.

"Need some help?" she asked, ignoring the guilty expressions on both women's faces. "I thought it must be time to set the table."

Twelve

A week after Thanksgiving, Erin looked up from the office window to see a trio of pickup trucks pull slowly into the parking area. They were black with a familiar logo on the side. Nick's trucks! She was almost too excited to notice that the second pickup was towing a small camp trailer behind it and the last one was pulling a flatbed on which two pieces of heavy yellow machinery were strapped down. One was a bulldozer, but Erin didn't recognize the other.

Trembling, she grabbed her coat and went outside. She expected to see Nick, but instead, a white-haired man in a denim jacket and a baseball cap climbed out of the first truck.

"I'm looking for Miss McKenzie," he said with a friendly smile.

Erin swallowed her disappointment. "I'm Erin McKenzie." More men were getting out of the trucks, three in all. They were dressed in work clothes and heavy boots, but Nick wasn't among them.

The man with the white hair offered his hand. "I'm Shorty Wills," he said. "I'm a foreman with Blackwood Construction in Eugene."

"I've been expecting you," Erin said. The permits had all been granted the week before.

"We're ready to start on your exercise wing."

"Is Nick coming later?" she asked.

Shorty shook his head. "No, ma'am. Nick's too busy in Eugene to take the time."

Her heart plummeted with disappointment, and she realized how much she had been counting on seeing him again. For a moment, she was afraid she was going to disgrace herself with tears.

"I've got the prints with me," Shorty added. "Nick sent his best crew. We'll do right by you." He must have seen the disappointment on Erin's face, but there was no way she could explain. Instead, she forced a smile.

"I have no doubt of that."

"Where can we park the field office?" Shorty asked, pointing at the little trailer. "I'd like it close to the job site."

Erin showed him where the addition was going in, and two of the men immediately began measuring and putting stakes in the ground. As she and Shorty were walking back to his truck, she mentioned the empty apartment units.

"You might as well all stay in them while you're here," she offered.

"We can find a motel," Shorty said, reminding Erin of Nick's words the first time they had met. "The company pays our expenses."

It took her a few minutes to convince him that the crew should stay at the center and take their meals in the dining hall. Since Nick was donating the labor and materials, Erin couldn't let him pay the crew's expenses, too. Finally Shorty asked to use her phone.

"There's one in the office," she said. "Come on." She waited while he made his call, keenly aware that Nick was on the other end of the line. She strained to hear his voice, then silently berated herself for being a lovelorn fool.

Nick was gone for good. He'd had a perfect excuse to come back and hadn't taken it. What more proof did she need that he was over her?

Vaguely, she heard Shorty ask about staying at the center. When he held the receiver out to Erin, it took her a moment to realize he meant for her to take it.

Nick wanted to speak to her.

She took the receiver with a hand that trembled.

"Hello?"

"Erin." His voice sounded so close! And so familiar that her knees threatened to buckle.

"Hello, Nick. Thank you for sending Shorty and the men."

"No problem. I'm glad they made good time. It's nice of you to offer to put the men up," he said.

"It's the least I can do," she replied, gripping the phone harder. "Besides, I'd feel better if they stayed here." If he could be strictly businesslike, so could she. "Wilma will be in heaven, cooking for men who look like they enjoy their food, and the apartment units are sitting empty, anyway."

There was silence on the other end. She wanted to ask how he had been, but didn't. She couldn't make herself say the words with Shorty standing there. She wanted to ask if he felt any better about Lucy living in Portland.

Instead, she merely said, "Let them stay here. I'd like to do that much, at least."

"Okay," Nick capitulated. "If you're sure. Thanks. Now, let me talk to Shorty again, will you?"

She gave the phone back. "I'll be outside," she said. He nodded and put the receiver to his ear.

When she left the office, Erin realized that she was shaking with reaction. She needed to regain her composure before she could face anyone, especially Nick's construction crew. She went around the corner and leaned against the wall, blinking back sudden tears. Then she took several deep breaths.

So much for the idea that she was getting over Nick. After that brief, impersonal exchange on the phone, she knew how utterly mistaken she had been.

* * *

Nick's crew went home for Christmas. Erin had sent cards to both him and Lucy from the staff at the center, the same cards she and Anna sent everyone who had ever come in contact with them. The holidays were an excellent time to remind people that they existed on donations.

Two days before Christmas, Erin got a large foil card that was printed on the inside with the name of Nick's company. There was no personal message. She wondered if Nick had sent it himself or had some secretary do it. Probably the latter.

She got a cute card with a mouse in a Santa hat sitting in a wheelchair on the front and a long letter from Lucy, who sounded as if she was working hard, making friends and adapting to her new life. She wrote that she and Max were going home for the week between Christmas and New Year's. Her parents were spending the holidays on a cruise ship, but Lucy and Nick would be celebrating at his house with friends.

Erin wondered if Nick's friends included anyone who was special to him. As she had once believed she was. As soon as the thought popped into her head, Erin was angry with herself. She ripped the card from Blackwood Construction in two, wadded up the heavy cream envelope and tossed them into the waste basket. And made a firm decision to put Nick out of her mind and enjoy the holidays. That would be her first New Year's resolution. An early one.

The crew finished in January. After everyone at the center raved about the addition, a large room that already contained several pieces of exercise equipment, an adjoining specially equipped hot tub area and a separate dressing room with showers, Erin thanked Shorty and the men once more. In no time, they had packed up and left.

"We need to have a dedication ceremony," Anna said. "Think of the publicity we'd get." Her eyes sparkled. "And the new contributors."

Erin knew that Anna was right. They made plans to have an Open House the next weekend.

"Are you going to call Nick or would you rather I did?" Anna asked.

"Nick?" Erin hated the tremor in her voice when she said his name.

Anna's smile was full of sympathy. "It would be nice to invite him," she said mildly. "And Lucy, too, of course."

"There's no reason to call," Erin said. "I need to write and thank him, so I'll just include an invitation with my note."

Anna's brows went up but she didn't say anything more. Erin sent the invitation and stayed on tenterhooks for the next week. Would he come to the Open House? If he harbored any wish to see her, he would. She told herself over and over that, if he refused, she would forget him once and for all.

And she wondered what she would say if he asked her again to go back with him.

Two days before the ceremony, Anna was sorting the mail. Wordlessly, she handed Erin an envelope embossed with Blackwood Construction's return address.

"I'm going to get some coffee," she said, rising and grasping her cane. "Do you want me to bring you back a cup?"

Erin tore her gaze from the envelope. "No, I guess not." She suspected that Anna was giving her privacy, that she had known all along what Erin was going through. She managed a smile. "Thanks, though."

"I hope it's good news." Anna squeezed her shoulder on her way out.

Erin tore open the envelope. She took a deep breath and unfolded the letter inside. At least it wasn't typed. It was politely worded, though, as polite as Erin's invitation had been. He appreciated the offer, and hoped the Open House was a big success, but he had to refuse with regret. He was just too busy with work to make the trip. He hoped she would understand. His foreman had given him a full report and he was glad Erin was pleased with the addition. If she had any problems or questions, he hoped she would feel free to let him know. Lastly, he wished her continued good luck with the center. He knew how much it meant to her.

She stared at that last sentence for a long time.

"Damn," she whispered softly. She had let him hurt her again. Then she began to get angry. Men! Why did a woman with a career intimidate them so? She had run into it over and over. Why had she ever expected Nick to be any different and to understand when others hadn't?

Nick gave Lucy a hug, patted Max on the head and quickly blinked away the moisture that threatened to blur his vision.

"Thanks for lunch," he said. "It was terrific."

"I'm glad you could come," she said.

After they ate, she had showed him proofs for her latest modeling assignment—on location at the zoo.

Now he cleared his throat and said something he knew he had put off for too long. "I'm truly proud of you, peanut," he said. "You've done so much better than I dreamed you could." He stopped and tried to swallow the suspicious lump in his throat. "I love you, baby."

She had tears in her eyes and so did he.

"I love you, too," she whispered, hugging him hard. "Thanks."

"I'll talk to you in a few days, okay?" he said. "Be thinking about who you want to invite to your party." She was going to be twenty in a few weeks, and he was throwing her a big party at his house. Another diversion. Another attempt to keep his mind off Erin. He already knew it wasn't going to work any better than anything else had.

"Now that I've begun to live my life, don't you think it's time you did the same?" Lucy demanded before he could turn away.

Nick's heart sank. "I'm living my life just the way I want," he replied, ignoring her expression of disbelief. Gently, he cuffed her chin. "Leave it alone, will you?"

She nodded but her smile was sad. "Okay."

"Thanks." He continued to do his best to ignore thoughts of Erin when he got home. As usual, only Sparky, his basset hound, was there to greet him. The housekeeper had left dinner in the oven, ready to heat in the microwave, and had gone home to her own family. Nick took a beer from the fridge, ignoring the food, and went into the den, Sparky at his heels.

Nick sat down at his desk and stared at the stack of work there. He had intended to oversee the addition to Erin's center in person, and then a big job in the outskirts of Portland began to go sour.

By the time Nick had straightened out the problems, it was too late for him to take over from Shorty.

Then Erin's stiff little note and the invitation to the Open House had arrived. He had battled with himself about going, had wanted to. And instead gave in to something he hardly ever did. His own fears.

Hearing her voice on the phone that one time Shorty called made Nick feel like his heart had been hacked out with a cleaver. Nothing had changed; he wasn't sure he could bear coming home without her again. It was easier not to see her at all.

Now he was still thinking about her when he cleared off his desk and found the set of plans he had been fooling around with before he left Monroe and had since forgotten about. He sat and stared at the rough sketches for a long time. The room grew darker as evening settled in. He switched on his desk lamp. Sparky came to inquire about his dinner but Nick didn't notice until the dog returned with his empty dish in his mouth and dropped it at Nick's feet. By then, he had moved to his drafting table and the rough drawings had begun to resemble real plans.

Lucy called the day after Erin got the invitation to her birthday party in the mail.

"Are you coming?" she demanded.

"I wish I could," Erin said, crossing her fingers. Wild horses couldn't have dragged her to Nick's house in Eugene. "I really can't get away."

There was a moment of silence. "I'm so disappointed," Lucy replied. It sounded like she was crying. "It would mean so much to me if you were there. You could see how well I'm doing."

"You'll be too busy to notice that I'm not," Erin said, feeling bad. "Perhaps I could come down to Portland for a visit later on."

"That just wouldn't be the same," Lucy sobbed. "You changed my life, and it just won't seem like a celebration without you."

Erin was at a loss. Flattered as well as dismayed. She had no idea she meant so much to Lucy. Yet how could she face Nick?

"You can stay at my parents' house," Lucy said. "They'll be back in town for the party and they asked me to invite you for them. You made such a good impression at my graduation."

Again, Erin was confused. She'd barely had time for two words with them. "Oh, I couldn't impose," she replied hastily.

"They'll be so disappointed if you don't," Lucy insisted. "It's a long drive, and you'll need a place to stay. They asked me to tell you to come anytime in the afternoon."

"I haven't said I could make it," Erin protested.

"You can change for the party at their house," Lucy continued.

Erin hesitated, nibbling her lip. She hated to spoil Lucy's birthday.

"Please," Lucy pleaded. It sounded like she was crying again. Erin's determination, which was already wavering despite a nagging inner voice, buckled.

"Oh, okay," she said, knowing she would live to regret the words. "If it means that much to you, I guess I could rearrange my schedule."

Lucy let out an ear-splitting "Yahoo!" that made Erin jerk the receiver away from her ear. "Oh, thank you, thank you," she cried. "You've made me so happy."

"I'm glad," Erin said weakly. It took so little to make some people happy.

"I'll tell the folks," Lucy continued enthusiastically. "I'm so pleased. You won't regret this."

Erin already regretted it. How had she let herself get talked into seeing Nick again, in his home, surrounded by his friends and, no doubt, with a date on his arm? Someone gorgeous and sophisticated. Erin decided she had to be crazy.

"Call me when you know what time you'll arrive," Lucy was saying. "I'll give you directions to Mom and Dad's. There's a map to Nick's house with the invitation."

"I noticed it," Erin replied grimly. If she could fish the pieces out of the wastebasket, she could probably tape them together. Otherwise, she would have to ask Nick's folks for directions.

"You can ride with us," Burt Blackwood suggested as he, Muriel and Erin gathered in the living room of their attractive rambler. He had already told Erin that Nick built it for them as an anniversary gift.

She had arrived an hour before and been shown to a guest room with its own bath. Now she waited nervously, holding Lucy's present, a pair of jade earrings, and wondering for the hundredth time why she had ever agreed to come.

"That's a lovely dress, dear," Muriel said. "Black is stunning with your hair, and those gold threads running through the material make it shimmer when you move."

Erin toyed with one of the gold hoops she was wearing. "Thank you." The dress was shorter than she usually wore. Her sheer panty hose and high heels showed off her legs and when she had first appeared, Burt embarrassed her by whistling.

"I think I'll take my own car," she said now. "But I'd like to follow you over." She wanted to be able to leave early if seeing Nick again was as much of a disaster as she suspected it would be.

"Shall we go?" Muriel suggested, handing Burt her coat. He helped her with it and then did the same for Erin as she tried to remain calm.

Nick's house, a majestic Tudor with two stories, was much more impressive than Erin had expected. What did one man do with all this room? she wondered as she stepped onto the circular brick driveway and an attendant parked her car.

For a moment, Erin feared that her shaky legs weren't going to hold her. Panic struck like an icicle through her heart and she couldn't draw breath. Wildly, she struggled for control, praying that no one would notice. She bit down hard on the inside of her cheek and dug her nails into her palms. By the time she had followed Burt and Muriel into the impressive entry and was facing Nick, the self-inflicted discomfort had done its work and she had regained a small measure of her equilibrium.

His gaze lingered on Erin long enough to make her knees shaky again, but he only thanked her for coming and asked if the drive down had been okay. He didn't extend his hand, and for that she was grateful. No doubt there was still a row of half-moons indented in each of her palms.

"The drive was uneventful," she replied to his question without adding how badly she had wanted to turn the car around.

Lucy, seated in her chair next to Nick, with Max at her side, was wearing a peach lace dress. A matching bow was tied to the handle of Max's harness. They both greeted Erin warmly before Lucy turned to the next group of arrivals.

"Let's talk later," she whispered to Erin.

Erin followed Burt and Muriel as they handed their coats to another attendant and went to the bar. She looked around while she waited for her usual diet soda. Tonight she would have preferred a double martini, except that she doubted she would have been able to stop after just one.

Glass in hand, she wandered past knots of people until she found a deserted sunroom at the back of the house. One wall and part of the ceiling were glass and potted plants almost filled the interior. There was a fountain in the middle of the room surrounded by white wrought iron furniture. Erin sat down and sipped her soda while she stared at the darkness beyond the glass—and wondered how soon she could leave.

Seeing Nick again had certainly been more painful than she had expected. She doubted her ability to carry off another meeting without disgracing herself.

"Here you are," Lucy said, startling her. Erin had no idea how long she had been sitting there alone. She rose guiltily from the bench.

"You look wonderful," she told Lucy. The glow of the peach dress was reflected in her cheeks. As usual, Max was with her. A basset hound Erin assumed must be Sparky approached her and sniffed her hand. Then he allowed her to scratch behind his ears while he made a rumbling sound of pleasure.

"Thanks," Lucy replied. "You look great, too." She extended her hand. "Come on," she said. "There are some people I want you to meet."

For the next hour, they made their way through the crush of guests, stopping frequently so that Lucy could introduce Erin and give the training center a plug.

Erin had frequent glimpses of Nick, but their paths didn't cross. He was always in the middle of some group, smiling and laughing. Once their gazes met briefly before Lucy dragged her on.

They entered a big, high-ceilinged room that had been cleared for dancing. A small band was set up in one corner and the overhead chandelier was dimmed. Lucy introduced Erin to a tall, attractive man named Allan, who promptly asked her to dance.

"Go ahead," Lucy said, smiling. "I see some late arrivals I need to say hello to."

Erin accepted the invitation with mixed feelings. Allan seemed nice enough, but she had planned on slipping away as soon as Lucy let her go.

The music was too loud for conversation, the beat fast. As soon as the number was over, Erin smiled at him and turned away. The band started a slow number and he caught her arm.

"Please?" he asked with an engaging smile.

Erin nodded and moved into his arms. She was explaining why she had come down for the party when she saw Nick from the corner of her eye. He tapped Allan's shoulder.

"Mind if I cut in?"

"Why should I let her go?" Allan demanded, grinning. Erin's mouth was dry, her pulse rate climbing.

"Because I sign your paycheck," Nick growled. "And you've monopolized the prettiest woman here for far too long."

"This is only our second dance," Allan protested.

Nick's expression was enigmatic. "Exactly."

Allan smiled and stepped back, releasing Erin's hand. "The man has a couple of valid points," he said cheerfully. "Maybe you'll save me another dance for later."

"And maybe not," Nick said.

Erin had no idea what she answered, or if she did. Nick held out his arms. She hesitated but it was only for effect. She knew that she couldn't resist. Knew now why she had accepted Lucy's teary pleas. Knew she was going to be hurt again, and hardly cared.

She moved into the circle of Nick's embrace. The music changed, slowed even more as if by prearranged signal. The two of them seemed to be floating in a bubble, separate from everyone else in the room.

"How have you been?" Nick asked as he guided her slowly around the floor.

"Just fine," she exclaimed brightly. "Busy, of course." Desperate to break the spell he was weaving around her before he saw past her pitiful defenses, she went on to chatter about the new addition and her future plans. She tried hard to avoid looking at him. He held her close and she was painfully aware of the heat and strength that radiated from his body to hers. She would have liked nothing more than to stay in his arms forever.

Finally, the dance was over. Their feet stopped moving but Nick didn't release her. Erin knew she had to break away, but she just couldn't make herself do it.

Nick leaned his forehead against hers. "I missed you." His voice was low and rough, as if the words had been torn from him without his permission.

Erin didn't respond. With mixed feelings, she finally moved away from him.

"Well," she said, anxious to make her escape before the music started again, "I think I'll check out the buffet table." The words were a lie. She planned to leave the party the moment his back was turned.

Nick frowned. "Would you come with me first? Just for a moment. There's something I'd like to show you."

"What?" she asked suspiciously. Surely not his etchings? Not at this point.

"Come and see." He took her hand and gently tugged on it.

Reluctantly, she agreed. He led her down a long hallway and opened a door. Erin followed him into what was obviously some kind of home office. The walls were paneled and lined with books. That was all she had time to notice before he pulled her into his arms.

She struggled. How dare he think he could kiss her as if the months apart had never happened.

He let her go immediately. "I'm sorry."

"Is this why you brought me in here?" she demanded. "For a little slap and tickle for old times' sake?"

He flushed and his eyes blazed. "No. Not totally. I do have something to show you."

She crossed her arms and waited. His gaze searched hers. "Have you missed me at all?"

There was something in his tone, and in his eyes, that cut through her defenses and her pride. Perhaps it was his pain calling out to hers. She didn't know. She only knew she couldn't stand there and pretend. Not now. This would probably be the last time she ever saw him. It was no longer important that she keep up a front, that he not know how she still felt.

She lowered her gaze and studied the toes of her shoes.

"Yes." Her voice was a ragged whisper, an admission freely given. "I've missed you."

The words were barely out before Nick wrapped his arms around her and lowered his head. Erin thought she heard him mutter "Thank God," right before he kissed her, but she couldn't be sure.

For a timeless moment, the world fell away, leaving only the two of them. Erin's head and heart were spinning out of control when he finally let her go. His eyes were glowing. She wondered if it was happiness she saw there. A reflection of her own momentary joy at being with him again.

Nick turned away and picked up a tube of paper from the drafting table that sat next to the massive oak desk. He began talking about some project his company was going to undertake. Only a slight tremor in his voice told Erin he had been affected as deeply as she had. Puzzled, she tried to concentrate while he unrolled a set of plans and began pointing things out.

"What do you think?" he asked, face intent.

She glanced at the squiggles and lines without comprehending them. Then a word caught her attention and she looked closer. The drawing was some kind of building complex.

Slowly, it dawned on Erin what she was looking at. The plans were for a training center, not unlike the one she had built in Monroe. As she studied the drawing through eyes suddenly misted with tears, she saw that the only differences seemed to be those she had described to Nick on their way back from one of her presentations.

She looked up, puzzled. "What does this mean?"

"Lucy's dog has changed the quality of her life," Nick said slowly. "Just like you promised it would. It took me a long time to see that. Longer to admit it. Even longer to work through my own guilt and the motives behind it. Now I want to build another center like yours here in Eugene."

"But how are you going to run it?" she asked. "What about the dogs and someone who knows how to train them?"

"I remember that woman I met at Lucy's graduation," he said. "Caroline. You told me she's a widow with time on her hands. And she knows how to train the dogs and teach the classes."

He wanted Caroline to relocate, to run this new center? Erin was speechless with shock. And envy.

"I don't know if Caroline would consider relocating," she said carefully. "But you could ask her. She's certainly qualified." Erin and Caroline had talked more than once about the possibility of Caroline taking over if Erin ever needed a replacement.

Nick's grin broadened, and another piece of Erin's heart broke off. "Do you think I want her to come here?" he asked.

Erin blinked with confusion. "Don't you?"

"Hell, no! I want her to take over in Monroe."

Something burst inside Erin's chest. "Monroe?" she echoed. "Why would you want her to do that?"

Nick's grin faded. She saw him swallow. He folded his hands around her upper arms and stared tensely into her face. A muscle in his cheek danced. "I want her to take over so the present director can relocate with her new husband." His voice was devoid of any expression. "And supervise the building of the new center down here."

The meaning behind his words began to soak in. Erin searched his face, which seemed to have gone pale.

The tears that had filled her eyes earlier threatened to spill over. "Why are you doing this?" she finally stuttered when she could find her voice.

Nick looked away. His own eyes had a suspicious sheen and his voice was raw with feeling. "Because my life has become a barren waste without you," he admitted. "Because I'd move Blackwood Construction to Monroe in a New York minute, but I'd be putting too many people out of work. People my father hired years ago, that I couldn't ask to relocate. Because I'd walk away in a blink and start over up there, but it would break my father's heart."

Nick looked down at her and she could see all that he was feeling in his eyes. "This is the only way I could come up with to make it work," he said. "Believe me, I've spent a lot of time thinking about it. If you were willing to come down here, supervise the construction, run the place like you did the one in Monroe—I know I'm asking a lot. Your parents are up there, your friends."

"But the man I love is here," Erin interrupted quietly.

Nick looked like she had just handed him the sun. Before he could speak, she threw her arms around his neck.

"I love you."

With a groan, he kissed her. Their lips fused, their hearts beating in unison. When they finally came up for air, he demanded, "You'll marry me?"

"Oh, yes." Her voice was very sure.

Nick let out a gusty sigh of relief. "Thank God!" he growled, and then he kissed her again. They were still oblivious to the rest of the world when the door flew open, bringing reality into the room along with Lucy and Max. Sparky followed, carrying his empty dish.

"Well, did it work?" Lucy demanded. "Did she say yes? Sorry, but I just couldn't wait in the hall any longer."

"You were in the hallway?" Erin asked.

Nick grinned down at her. "Did it work?" he asked.

"You betcha," Erin whispered as the tears ran down her cheeks. Nick's smile was crooked and Lucy began dabbing at her eyes.

"This is the best present the two of you could give me," she said. "I always suspected it would take a headstrong redhead to tame my stubborn brother. Once I met you, Erin, I knew it was just a matter of time."

"I wish you had let me in on your revelation," Erin exclaimed dryly as both Lucy and Nick chuckled. "It would have saved me a few bad moments over the last three months."

"Only a few?" Nick asked.

She gave him a look but didn't reply.

"Thanks for getting her down here," he told Lucy.

Erin stared as the light began to dawn. "All that begging and crying?" she asked. "You mean it wasn't true?"

"Of course it was," Lucy said. "But desperate times call for desperate measures," she added self-righteously. "And you were a hard sell."

"What if I hadn't agreed?" Erin asked.

Before Lucy could speak, Nick said, "Then I would have had to come up and get you. This way just saved me a trip."

She pretended to swat at him, but she was too happy to take offense. As Lucy watched, beaming, Nick scooped Erin into his arms and spun her around. "Let's go tell my folks," he said.

"Were they in on this, too?" she asked.

Nick didn't answer but his grin showed no remorse. He whirled her around again as Lucy applauded. Sparky dropped his dish and began to bark.

COMING NEXT MONTH

#9 ALL ABOUT EVE *by Patty Copeland*
Eve Sutton was just an hour away from her destination when her car sputtered to a halt. And a stranded tourist was the very last thing Dr. Adam Wagner needed.

#10 THE CANDY DAD *by Pat Pritchard*
A down-to-earth single suburban mom was hardly his type but Jesse Daniels couldn't deny the sweet fantasies Rennie Sawyer inspired.

#11 BROKEN VOWS *by Stephanie Daniels*
When Wendy Valdez' smile melted his heart, Jack O'Connor didn't know how to respond. It would be easy to fall—fast and hard—for this tempting woman.

#12 SILENT SONG *by Leslie Knowles*
Nicole Michael couldn't believe it was him. Had Jake Cameron discovered the reason she'd left him so abruptly?

Plus four other great romances!

AVAILABLE THIS MONTH:

#1 PERFECT MATCH
Pamela Toth

#2 KONA BREEZE
Darcy Rice

#3 ROSE AMONG THORNES
Pamela Macaluso

#4 CITY GIRL
Mary Lynn Dille

#5 SILKE
Lacey Dancer

#6 VETERAN'S DAY
GeorgeAnn Jansson

#7 EVERYTHING ABOUT HIM
Patricia Lynn

#8 A HIGHER POWER
Teresa Francis